"All I want to do i

"…and I don't know if you want that or not. Do you?" Automatically, Colt's breath hitched.

Touched by his sudden vulnerability, Shelly hesitated. The specter of making mistakes with men in the past made her freeze. She shouldn't do this. And yet, her heart screamed to reach out. Blindly, Shelly lifted her hand and slid it across his cheek. Mistake or not, she followed her pounding heart.

"Yes, I'd like to kiss you, Colt."

Shocked by her admittance, Colt felt her lips settle against his own. Shelly's mouth was soft and pliant.

Groaning internally, Colt swept his arms around Shelly and brought her fully against him. He captured her and tasted her. Just the grazing touch of her soft skin against his sent a keen ache through him. Fire ignited within as he deepened their kiss….

Books by Lindsay McKenna

LINDSAY McKENNA

As a writer, Lindsay McKenna feels that telling a story is a way to share how she sees the world. Love is the greatest healer of all, and the books she creates are parables that underline this belief. Working with flower essences, another gentle healer, she devotes part of her life to the world of nature to help ease people's suffering. She knows that the right words can heal and that creation of a story can be catalytic to a person's life. And in some way she hopes that her books may educate and lift the reader in a positive manner. She can be reached at www.lindsaymckenna.com or www.medicinegarden.com.

USA TODAY Bestselling Author

LINDSAY McKENNA

━━∽∾∽━━

THE ADVERSARY

Silhouette Books

n⚫cturne™

SILHOUETTE BOOKS

ISBN-13: 978-0-373-61834-7

Recycling programs
for this product may
not exist in your area.

THE ADVERSARY

www.silhouettenocturne.com

Printed in U.S.A.

Dear Reader,

How can two people from different cultures ever understand one another, much less learn to work together as a well-oiled team?

Shelly Godwin from Canmore, Canada, is a very famous vortex hunter. Colt Black, at twenty-eight years old, is a Navajo medicine man in training from Arizona. A series of dreams brings them together for a life-changing meeting in Banff.

I had great fun going to Banff National Park in Canada. There are few places on Earth that can rival the mystical beauty of the Rocky Mountains in this park. Since most of the action takes place in Banff, I had to hike in a lot of places to ensure that I was describing them accurately.

I loved writing this book, a part of the continuing series of WARRIORS FOR THE LIGHT. I had the most fun showing how our terribly mistake-ridden human side impacts others and situations far into the future. Enjoy!

Warmly,

Lindsay McKenna

Chapter 1

Six-year-old Colt Black froze, hiding the fact that he was shaking. He lay near a thin-paned window that had been built into the plaster, mud and timber of the hogan built by his Navajo grandparents. It was a warm summer night. The son of a famous medicine man, Colt couldn't show fear—ever. Medicine men were considered courageous. Heroic. Powerful. But fear rippled through him like the evil lightning that often came in the summer thunderstorms to stalk the Navajo reservation. Navajos feared two things—being struck by lightning and getting bitten by a rattlesnake. If bitten or struck, the person was sent away from their family forever. No one wanted the curse of bad energy hanging around.

This time it wasn't the thunder that had awakened him. His parents had brought the family to visit his father's parents. His sister, Mary, a year younger than him, slept with her back next to Colt. They were all in the large hogan. During his family's visit, his father, Harvey Black, had placed him at the low window to sleep. Big mistake as something had awakened Colt. Rubbing his eyes, he saw the moon shining brightly through the small, dusty window.

A face suddenly appeared at the window, and a scream lodged in Colt's throat. Through wide, shocked eyes he stared at the coyote and man who seemed to be melded together into one head and body.

It was a Skin Walker!

This was the most feared of all the sorcerers on the Navajo reservation. Colt's father was a medicine man of good standing and fine reputation. But there were others who wanted only domination and didn't care about helping. They were witches who worked with the dark side of energy. These men lusted after power and unconditional control. They could shape-shift into the body of a coyote and possessed super-human strength. Skin Walkers prowled through the night in hopes of possessing the soul of a human who had been caught outdoors after dark.

Colt should have felt safe but he didn't. He was

unable to move as his gaze met the glittering, gleaming eyes of the Skin Walker. The monster's mouth opened and he smiled. The canines of a coyote-man dripped with saliva. He pressed his muzzle against the glass, his nose flattening against it.

No! Colt tried to move. Terror and chills worked up his spine. The eyes of the Skin Walker continued to stare into him. Lips lifted away from its teeth in a savage grimace. Colt's young mind screamed. His mouth worked, but nothing came out. He was truly paralyzed, a captive of this grisly sorcerer.

His small hands clenched into fists as the Skin Walker's entire head filled the window. Where his black nose pressed hard and flattened against the glass, puffs of moisture came and went. Only a quarter of an inch separated them. If only Colt could cry out for help. His father's snoring reminded him that he was nearby. Why didn't his father wake up? He was a medicine man with powerful paranormal sight, a great healer among their people. Mind frantic, Colt could only stare at the snarling mouth, the yellowed teeth and the dripping saliva.

It was then that Skin Walker lifted his paw; his nails were long, jagged and gnarled. Colt stared at them, mesmerized. The high, screeching sound of claws scraping against glass continued at the window. Savagely, the Skin Walker tried to claw through it to get at Colt. Instinctively, Colt thrust out his hand and touched his sister Mary's hip. She was asleep. Didn't she feel the evil of the Skin Walker who wanted to possess him?

His heart was beating so wildly in his chest he thought it would pop. Why didn't anyone wake up? And then, a scream finally lurched out of Colt's mouth. It was a high, truncated shriek. Mary stirred and instantly joined in, disoriented and frightened.

The whole family awakened, but not soon enough, for Colt caught the Skin Walker silently mouthing a curse at him. In seconds, it disappeared from the window, dust rising in the wake of its departure.

Now, many years later, Colt jerked awake, quickly sitting up on his pallet, the light sheet pooling around his hips. He was sweating, his heart pounding. He shakily pushed his fingers through his short hair and tried to forget the savage glitter in the Skin Walker's eyes. The nightmare had stalked him at least once a week since that horrible night. His life had been forever changed by that experience. Looking up, Colt watched the moonlight leaking through the gauzy curtains across the three windows of his small hogan. It was summer. He'd opened the windows, the screens were in place. No one drove or walked outside at night. When the sun went down, people were inside, doors locked against the roving Skin Walkers who moved like silent, deadly shadows across the desert landscape.

Another ugly scene arose from his memory. Mary…his little sister. Something life-changing had happened the following week after the Skin Walker had come to the window of the hogan and tried to get at Colt and his sister.

Their father, Harvey Black, was late getting back from a ceremony. He'd taken Colt and Mary with him since he wanted his children to see what he did. Their pickup had coughed, sputtered and rolled to a stop on a dirt road. Harvey had tried several times to get it to start, but the engine was dead.

Terrified when his father had left them in the pickup as darkness fell, Colt was charged with keeping the windows up, the doors locked and Mary safe. A friend's hogan was a mile down the road and Harvey was going there for help.

Colt hadn't dared ask his father about the Skin Walkers. He was too ashamed after his screaming a week earlier. Instead, Colt sat stiffly, his arms around Mary in the hot, stuffy truck cab. He'd watched the dusk deepen and sink into the ink of the night. Colt couldn't see the beauty of the stars twinkling overhead. No. He felt a Skin Walker nearby. Stalking them. The man-animal laughed to himself in glee that he had two victims to possess.

Rubbing his face, Colt sighed as he tried to erase the horror of that night. It was impossible. The Skin Walker on silent pads approached from the rear of the truck. Colt felt him coming. Mary was asleep in his arms, completely unaware of the danger they were in. Suddenly, the coyote shape-shifter lifted his lips in a snarl and placed his yellow fangs against the driver's-side window. With his claws, he worked to open the door. Colt went into shock.

The Skin Walker howled, laughed. Drool came out of the sides of his mouth as he walked around the truck again and again. He clawed at the windows, halted, then pulled on the locked door latch. The pickup shook with the power of his efforts to get to them.

Colt sat there, mouth pursed, his arms tight around Mary, heart pounding. The nightmare didn't seem as if it would ever end.

Finally, the Skin Walker, who had tried every way to get into the truck, got impatient. Shape-shifting back into a human, he cursed them in Navajo, left and then returned with a huge rock in his hands.

To his everlasting terror, Colt watched the rock smash through the driver's-side window. It cracked into thousands of weblike lines. The Skin Walker's laugh and howl made every hair on Colt's body stand up. With one hard smack of the sorcerer's palm, the window burst into the cab, scattering like hundreds of shattered diamonds all over them. After shape-shifting back into a coyote, the Skin Walker reached in and dragged Mary to the other side of the pickup. Colt screamed and tried to place himself in front of her.

In moments, the Skin Walker had jerked open the door. Colt would never forget the rotting, dead odor around the coyote, those wild yellow eyes. As much as he could, he kept kicking at the monster. Mary pressed up against him and the door, crying out.

Colt felt the hot sting of the Skin Walker's fingernails as he raked them across his cheek. Though frightened, he felt no pain. All he wanted to do was stop the Skin Walker from taking both of them. The survival instinct gave him the courage to combat the sorcerer. But nothing stopped the Skin Walker from looming inside the cab, his narrowed eyes fixed on Mary. *No!*

Even as Colt tried to fight back, the Skin Walker snarled and struck Colt in the face. A terrible crunching sounded inside Colt's head. The blow was so powerful, it knocked him unconscious.

When he came to later, his father and his friend stood panicked over him. *Mary was gone!* Colt tried to tell them everything, but his front teeth had been knocked out, his mouth was swollen. It was the only time he'd heard his father scream and then begin to sob. In the end, they'd found Mary two days later, after a massive search, dead upon the slopes of a mesa where the Skin Walker was known to live. Shortly after that, his father had taken a rifle, stalked the witch and shot him dead. No one on the reservation ever told law enforcement anything. But everyone knew that his father had killed the male witch known as Yellow Teeth.

Colt had never forgiven himself since that night. He should have protected Mary more. If he had, she would be alive today.

Getting up, the moonlight gleaming against his naked body, he walked over to the small kitchen counter and poured himself a glass of water.

As he drank, the cooling liquid refreshed him. He set the glass down on the counter and glanced at his watch. It was 1:00 a.m. and he had to get back to sleep.

As he settled back down on his pallet and pulled the sheet up to his waist, Colt closed his eyes. The fear had dissolved. How long was this nightmare going to follow at his heels? He was twenty-eight years old. It was ridiculous, he thought, that this same nightmare could trail him for so long. Sighing softly, he punched the pillow and lay on his side, his back to the windows.

As the son of a famous Navajo medicine man, Colt couldn't speak of his horrors. He'd learned his lesson. Way back when, his father had laughed that night when he'd heard the story from Colt, saying it had only been a dream. Looking back on it, that first visit to the hogan was only the beginning. Yellow Teeth had targeted Colt and Mary and wanted to possess them.

Because Colt didn't want to sleep by that window, he'd cried. He wanted to curl up against his mother. She had already taken weeping Mary in her arms and had allowed her to sleep beside her after the incident. Disappointed, his father scolded him, stressing that he was a young man now and no longer had the luxury of a mother's arms to protect him. After all, Colt was the first-born son and was expected to show courage, not cowardice, in the face of such danger.

Harvey shook his finger in Colt's face and told him he was a coward. Only one without courage screamed in the face of fear—real or not. Colt was forced by his disappointed father to lie back down facing that same window. When he awoke the next morning, they had a naming ceremony for him: Colt Runs Away. In Navajo society, one was given a name after birth, but it could be changed at any time depending upon events in a person's life. Well, at six years old Colt had been renamed and *coward* was whispered on the lips of all his relatives from that time onward.

This was danger mixed with violence, threat and raw evil, but it made no difference to his family. Lying here now, as an adult, Colt went through the entire scenario again as he had thousands of times before. His father had told him from an early age that Skin Walkers were male witches who possessed a coyote spirit in order to possess a person. And once possessed, that person became zombielike. They drifted like detached, lifeless ghosts through their lives. Outsiders would say they were addicted to drugs by their vacant-eyed stare, their inability to feel or react to any emotions. They all died unnatural and early deaths. Colt shivered internally. At six years old, actually seeing a Skin Walker through the window had driven the terror home.

Colt had not wanted to follow in his father's footsteps because it was well-known that sorcerers constantly battled medicine men for supremacy on the reservation. There was a shield to protect a medicine man from possession and his father had taught Colt how to protect himself. Raw courage in the face of such evil was expected of him.

Everyone's courage had been tested the night Yellow Teeth had stolen and killed Mary. Colt grew up hounded by Yellow Teeth in spirit. Skin Walkers were just as powerful without a body. To this day Colt had to keep the bubble of protection around himself twenty-four hours a day or the shape-shifter would attack and possess him.

His last thought was to keep up the shield of protection against evil in general and against possession and sorcery in particular. Colt was saved from further mental anguish because he fell into a deep sleep.

The dream started out like fog stealing quietly across the landscape of his mind. Colt found himself standing in a grassy, wildflower-strewn bank with thick fir trees on the high side of the sloping area. A few feet below an oval turquoise lake glittered like a jewel amongst the snow-clad mountains surrounding him. It was morning; the sun was warm on his body. Above, a few puffy clouds floated in the sky. He heard the sharp, short call of a woodpecker in a nearby fir and saw it fly down to the lake and disappear into another tree stand near a rocky bank.

What was this place? Colt could wake up within his dream and explore. His father called it *lucid dreaming* and it was a skill that ran through the family's bloodline. As he turned around, Colt noticed human activity above him. Hikers on a forest trail walked toward a one-story rock building just a few feet above the lake where he stood. He smelled frying bacon and fresh hot coffee. This cabin appeared to be a restaurant. Hikers climbed the wooden steps and came out with their food and paper cups filled with steaming coffee. The laughter, the smiles of the people made Colt feel good. He liked the place's energy.

And then, a young woman came down the well-trodden trail toward the restaurant. She had shoulder-length red hair and the most vivid hazel eyes he'd ever seen. She was beautiful in a natural way, and Colt was mesmerized by her grace as she walked along the trail above him. She was alone. Tall and curvy, she carried a yellow backpack, a dark green baseball cap shaded her eyes and a camera was hung around her neck. A set of formfitting jeans and a bright red T-shirt outlined her long legs and lush curves. She had to be just a few inches shorter than his six feet. Most of all, as she drew closer, Colt liked the blanket of freckles across her cheeks. Her skin was flushed from exertion at this altitude. His heart lurched. How badly he wanted to talk with this woman.

Something pushed Colt to do just that. As a Navajo he had been taught to try to walk in harmony and not to be the proverbial bull in the china shop. Being pushy wasn't built into his demeanor. Not until now. As he hurried up the bank and onto the trail, Colt's heart hammered with fear of rejection along with unparalleled excitement.

"Hey," Colt called, lifting his hand. "I'm Colt Black. Who are you?"

The woman stopped, smiling as he drew near her. "I've been waiting to meet you, Colt."

Stunned by her comment, Colt stared at her. "You were?"

"Yes." She turned and pointed down at the lake. "We have to find the emerald sphere. It's in the area of a vortex in a lake shaped like this. Are you ready? There's a sorcerer who wants it, too, and he would kill for it." She searched his eyes, her face serious, her gaze intent. "Will you go with me, Colt? I can't do this alone. You are my chosen partner on this important journey."

"An emerald sphere?" Colt wondered what this was all about.

"Yes, the world needs it. Only you can help me."

"But, you said a sorcerer would try to kill us if we looked for it?" Instantly, Yellow Teeth's narrowed face, feral yellow eyes and drooling mouth appeared to Colt. Being hunted by a sorcerer was nothing new to him. Was Yellow Teeth the sorcerer going after this sphere in her dream?

"As a team, we can protect one another. We have to find it before he does." Her lips pursed, she searched his face. "Please come with me. I can't do this by myself."

Colt wondered if this woman really understood the constant threat of this deadly sorcerer. Even a beautiful dream like this was disintegrating before the evil of his nemesis, Yellow Teeth. Her auburn brows knitted and he sensed her disappointment. Colt tried to think of a polite way to speak about the Skin Walker to her.

"You're afraid," she accused.

The words hit Colt like ice. There was a note of challenge in her green, brown and gold eyes. Her voice was soft but husky, with a hint of steel behind it. She had courage to call him a coward.

"You don't know what you're talking about," he muttered. In some ways, she reminded him of Mary, so vulnerable and innocent.

She eyed him intently. "Oh, yes, I do."

"I'm not the one you're seeking." A protective instinct arose in him and he feared for this woman's life. Didn't she know the danger Yellow Teeth harbored? He didn't want this lovely young woman harmed. The Skin Walker had told him many times that he would stalk him from the spirit world and someday, when Colt did not have his protection in place, he would kill him just as he'd killed his little sister.

"You're exactly who I'm looking for." She pushed her index finger into his chest to emphasize her words. Her eyes grew fierce as she held his gaze. "You have a strong heart. You stand for the quiet goodness that we're all seeking in this world. You're the one I've come to meet and no one else will do. I know your courage even if others cannot see it."

Colt searched the woman's large, beautiful eyes. Her mouth, full and soft-looking, lifted at the corners. "You don't want me for this mission."

"Your heart is pure. A strong heart full of good-ness is the only antidote against sorcery and evil. Love conquers everything, even sorcerers. No, you're the one I want at my side."

Her fervent, emotional plea touched him deeply. He continued to watch her, trying to figure out who she was. Colt thought she might be in her mid-twenties. The wind touched her hair and it moved restlessly across her proud shoulders. Her feistiness and courage shook Colt to his roots. He wanted to be with her. A new kind of strength flooded him.

"How am I to meet you?" he asked, regretting that he only wanted to continue this new alliance. How could he involve this woman in his ugly, fes-tering world of terror and violence?

She grinned. "You need to get into your car and drive here, to Banff National Park in Canada. I will meet you at the Château Lake Louise at 3:00 p.m. five days from now. That will be July fifth."

"But…what is your name?"

The dream faded and Colt awoke with a jolt. This had been one of those dreams he had heard about from medicine men. A cosmic signpost that guided a person toward some important and life-changing event.

Sitting up, Colt crossed his legs and pulled the sheet up around his waist. Everything was quiet. He could hear an owl somewhere out on the darkened reservation calling for his mate. Frowning, Colt took a hard look at himself. Maybe this was an opportunity to change his life. He scowled and studied the Navajo rugs across the floor of his hogan. They had been woven by his mother, grandmother and aunts over the years. He wished for the comfort of family through this next journey. Most of all, he wanted to prove that he was better than the child who ran away in fear of a sorcerer.

Was this beautiful white woman real or just part of a dream sent by a Yei, a Navajo god or goddess? Colt eased to his feet. He struck a match and lit a kerosene lamp on the table. After placing the globe over the flame, he walked over to a small desk. He drew out a paper and pen and wrote down everything he recalled from the dream. This was one time he wished for a phone, but none was available in his area.

The most obvious truth from the dream was how magnetically drawn he was to this red-haired white woman with the freckles on her cheeks. She was natural and without makeup. Putting the pen aside, he folded the piece of paper. He would drive his pickup to Flagstaff, Arizona, about fifty miles away and go to a library. There, Colt was sure he'd find the information to show his dream had some basis in reality.

He leaned against the counter and stared off into

the semidarkness within the hogan. More than any-thing, he wanted to change his life. After carrying the weight of a Skin Walker, he was ready for a change.

He opened his wooden trunk, drew out a pair of clean jeans and a white cotton long-sleeved cowboy shirt. As he dressed, Colt decided to drive to Flag-staff as soon as dawn broke. Until the night was chased away by Father Sun, Skin Walkers and ghosts ruled the land. No one dared step out of their hogan.

The thrill of unexpected adventure flowed through Colt. He hadn't felt this alive—ever. What if this red-haired woman was real? His heart burst open with a rush of joy. Could this dream, this woman, bring him a life filled with light instead of constant darkness? He silently thanked the Yei for sending him this dream of hope. And perhaps the Yei, in their benevolence, were giving him a way to change his fortune and future on the reservation by hunting for this emerald sphere. With her…

Chapter 2

Shelly Godwin wasn't sure if the instructions in her dream were real or not. She stood on the patio near the Château Lake Louise. The July day was very warm for the Canadian Rockies and she absorbed the welcome sunlight. Lake Louise's turquoise water shimmered like a blue jewel in the midday sun.

She wasn't sure what the dream meant. After pushing her red hair off her shoulders, she quickly tied the strands back into a ponytail. Who was this mysterious man she'd invited to meet her here? Shelly had had two dreams. In the first she asked this stranger to come on a mission with her. She'd had a second dream the following night, in which she was told to come to this hotel in Banff National Park in Alberta, Canada. She was to meet the stranger here at this hotel at 3:00 p.m. on July fifth.

She looked at her watch. It was almost time. Who was he and would he show up? Burned by a lifetime of failed relationships with men, Shelly wasn't sure she wanted to team up with another man for any reason. Yet, her prophetic dreams had never led her astray. She came from a long line of Irish seers and her generational DNA had given her the ability not only to have foretelling dreams but also to find vortexes.

Why on earth would she dream of a man? Terrence, the last failure, had hurt her terribly. She had written a book called *Find a Vortex.* It had become an instant global bestseller, much to her surprise. Terrence had come into her life to use her and try to ride the coattails of her fame. Shaking her head, Shelly still felt anger that she hadn't seen his true colors. All he'd wanted to do was use her name and manipulate her into writing a sequel of which he would be the co-author—in name only. *The bastard!* When would she learn not to trust men? The lessons had been hard, and now Shelly was gun-shy.

Pursing her tense lips, Shelly continued to look at the people coming and going from the chic and expensive hotel. Lake Louise was famous and she saw all kinds of people in hiking gear, all rich enough to pay for such a stay. Oh, she had the money, too. Her book had catapulted her into the domain of the rich and famous. She had gone from eking out a living to being very, very rich. And she liked it. But now she had a new challenge. This new man.

Snorting softly, Shelly rubbed her hands down her jeans and kept watch.

She remembered from one of the dreams that he was dressed like a cowboy.

Rubbing her arms, Shelly frowned. Was she ready for this? Only a year had passed since she'd booted Terrence out of her life. Since then, Shelly had holed up and kept to herself. She continued giving lectures around the world on how to find a vortex, what it was and how to work with one if it was discovered. Her publisher was happy with her. At every lecture, a hundred or more people came, and they all bought her book. She had rebuilt her life. So why did she feel as if it was all about to change?

Turning on the heel of her hiking boot, Shelly kept searching the sea of people walking up and down the smooth flagstone patio that led up to the hotel.

All this because of two crazy dreams! Shelly was used to dreams from her guides. Her parents had taught her from an early age that her guides—or what some might call their guardian angels—would help her throughout her life. Her dreams had always come true, so she had no reason to doubt these recent ones. They just didn't make sense.

She thought more deeply about the man she'd seen in the dream. He was a ruggedly handsome cowboy dressed in a white cotton shirt and blue jeans. He was sinfully good-looking in a rugged way. What had made him seem dangerous were the four scars across his left cheek, as if someone with long nails had raked his flesh. He had a hardness about him. Where did it come from? She could see it in the way his mouth thinned, the narrowed look in his intense blue eyes. He was awfully standoffish. The sense of danger swirling around him was palpable. And yet she felt no manipulative energy around him. Did it matter? As much as she trusted no man, she couldn't help but want to know more about this cowboy.

At the end of the dream, she was told her partner would bring the rest of the information. They could piece it together and get an understanding of why they had been brought together on this sacred mission.

The idea intrigued Shelly. A mission. An important one. One that could help the Earth. She was always eager to do anything that could uplift the environment. That was what had made her drive from her home in Canmore, a town just outside the park, here to Lake Louise. Pure curiosity about this mysterious mission had drawn her. Not entirely the man, although Shelly had liked his looks. Again, she looked at her watch. Time was crawling by. Were her dreams really going to come true? She'd know shortly.

COLT BLACK PARKED HIS rental car in the hotel's lot and got out. He stood in the hot July afternoon sunshine, his curiosity level high. He took his black Stetson out of the car and settled it on his head. It was 2:30 p.m.; he had enough time to just stand and open up to the energy of this place. It had taken a lot for him to get from his Navajo reservation to Canada. His conscience smarted.

He'd told his powerful medicine-man father about his dreams and he had urged him to come to Banff. His mother, who was a white woman and teacher on the reservation, had agreed with her husband. When his relatives had found out about it, they became angry. Who would continue to give them money for food? Colt held a part-time construction job in Flagstaff. While he did get paid for conducting ceremonies on his reservation, it wasn't enough to feed his needy relatives. Some family members had accused him of being selfish. Was he being selfish? It was too late now.

As he scanned the busy parking lot, Colt noticed the huge hotel in the distance. He was used to living on the spare Southwestern desert near Chinle, Arizona. The dream had shown him this hotel and the name above the front entrance. In a second dream, an ancient yet youthful Yei goddess had given him more instructions. The Yei had told him it was important he meet the red-haired woman at 3:00 p.m.

It all seemed strange. This was the first time in Colt's twenty-eight years of life that he'd ever traveled outside of the U.S.A. His work, his focus, was on the Navajo reservation where he'd been born and lived.

This was different. All of it. He admired the lush greenness of the firs, the mighty Rocky Mountains clothed at their peaks with white snow, their blue granite sides and their lower slopes clothed in evergreen trees. He always loved going to Flagstaff, the nearest large town to the Arizona part of the Navajo reservation, where the Grandmothers, a set of four mighty peaks that rose to fourteen thousand feet, stood above the town. Colt enjoyed his job as a boss of a construction team there because of the coolness at seven thousand feet, the lush trees and shrubs. Where he lived there was desert and plenty of rocks, cactus, red earth and beautiful, towering buttes. But there were no trees like this. Just Juniper, a scrubby, short tree.

Would the red-haired woman of his dreams be here to meet him? Colt looked around. Sometimes he saw the spirit of the Skin Walker in the distance, hiding and watching him. Would Yellow Teeth be here, as well? Even though he didn't sense his nemesis yet, Colt couldn't relax. The moment he did, Yellow Teeth would come in and try to possess him. As always, Colt was enclosed in the energy bubble of protection.

Swallowing hard, Colt made his face unreadable. As he watched people driving in and out of the large parking lot, he felt completely out of place. Dressed in his Southwestern clothing, he didn't blend in at all with the tourists. The cars were new and many were very expensive models compared to the small blue Toyota Prius he had rented at the Calgary airport.

Colt sauntered toward the hotel in the distance, tension tight in his gut. Jays swept around and squawked at him. They, too, seemed to warn him. Jays only cried out in alarm when a threat was imminent. Despite this, he tried to enjoy the wildflowers along the edge of the lot, their heads waving in an inconstant breeze. Most of all, he deeply inhaled the pine-scented air into his lungs. Trying to subdue his curiosity, Colt stepped onto the broad concrete sidewalk and continued toward the magnificent modern hotel.

Part of him was interested and the other was as excited as a little boy. This was a great adventure, his father had told him. One had to follow one's dreams wherever they led. Still, Colt worried about his relatives. His father had told him they would manage without him until he could fulfill the demand of his dreams: to find this woman. Who was she? He had information to share with her. Nothing had prepared him for this moment in his life.

"RENO, I DON'T KNOW what's wrong." Calen stood in the mission room of the Vesica Pisces foundation in Quito, Ecuador. She looked at her Apache husband who sat at the desk. "Why am I not getting a dream about where the next sphere is located?"

Reno heard the concern in his wife's voice and, rising, walked over to her. "I don't know, Calen." He slid his arms around her and pulled her against him. After pressing a kiss to her hair, he said in a gruff tone, "Maybe because Robert Cramer was killed on the last mission and the sorcerer Guerra stole the emerald sphere? Or that Victor Guerra, the Dark Lord of the *Tupay,* has it now? Was he able to find out through the spirit of the emerald where the next one is and where to look for it?"

With a muffled sound of frustration, Calen leaned back enough to search Reno's cinnamon-colored eyes. "I feel so guilty. I feel as though we've failed everyone. What about the other emerald spheres still out there? What is going to happen to them? If I don't get a dream about where the next one is, we're in trouble."

Nodding, Reno said, "I know. Maybe because Guerra stole the fourth sphere, the spheres have set up a different energy pattern. We just need to be patient, Calen."

"I feel that they're punishing us. Not that we don't deserve it." Sun shot through the floor-to-ceiling windows in their office planning room. "We lost Robert Cramer because we didn't do our job."

Reaching out, Reno slid his large copper hand down the length of her back. It was July, winter in Quito, Ecuador. "We did the best we could," he soothed, his voice a rumble. "No one said finding all seven emerald spheres was going to be easy. We made a mistake in choosing Robert for the last mission. He really wasn't up to it on a clairvoyant level, but we didn't know it at the time." Giving Calen a slight smile, Reno added, "We're doing the best we can, Calen. We knew there were going to be challenges. Victor Guerra is turning up the heat. He's already got one of the seven emerald spheres. There are three left to find." Reno left the rest unsaid: that without all seven spheres the Emerald Key necklace could not be restrung and worn by

Ana, the daughter of the sorcerer who now was working with them.

Glumly, Calen said, "I know…and there's no way to get it out of the *Tupay* stronghold, either. We can't just waltz in there and take it. No *Taqe* is allowed in there, just as no *Tupay* is allowed into our sacred and protected Village of the Clouds."

Reno squeezed her gently. "Listen, there's something going on that we don't know about. I feel the Great Spirit is still helping us, but maybe in a different way. Guerra has gotten too used to the way we did business. We didn't change tactics. We became too sure of ourselves. That's why we lost Cramer and the emerald. I don't believe we're being punished to the extent that we'll never be able to find the other spheres."

She gazed over at her husband, his black hair framing his Apache face. How much she loved this man. Despite the rugged look of his weathered face, his heart was tender and giving. "Okay, I'll kick myself out of my blues."

"We have to maintain our hope," Reno told her. "Even in the darkest hours, we have to hold that energy. Only by doing that will we be successful in the end."

Calen nodded and knew he was right. "I'm just worried. I always got a dream showing me where the next emerald sphere was going to be."

"Let's just see what develops over the next couple of weeks. That's all we can do." He gazed deep into her worried eyes.

SHELLY FELT HIS APPROACH. She turned, and her eyes widened. Coming up the walk with several other tourists was a copper-skinned cowboy wearing a black Stetson. It was him! Her heart started to beat rapidly and Shelly pressed her hand to her chest. How ruggedly good-looking he was. His hardness, a wall that let no one in, hit her full force. She saw the four claw-mark scars on his left cheek. He was even more devastatingly handsome than in her dream. He wore a white cotton cowboy shirt with long sleeves rolled up to just below his elbows. A black leather vest emphasized his broad chest. The faded, well-worn blue jeans and a pair of scuffed cowboy boots presented a picture of a man who routinely worked in the elements. The energy around him was strong. She'd never met anyone like him before.

When he looked up and their eyes met, she felt as if she'd just gotten an electric shock. His eyes were the same startling blue color as in her dream. His square face and high cheekbones clearly showed his Native American descent. Shelly guessed that he had some Caucasian blood in order to have those blue eyes. Most of all, Shelly liked his full mouth, the corners slightly curved. Right now, that mouth was tight, as if holding back emotion. He seemed to study her.

Shelly tried to push away her excitement. The past haunted her and although she was powerfully drawn to this man, she couldn't forget all she'd endured. As he sauntered toward her, Shelly's mouth went dry. Their eyes stayed locked and an incredible wave of heat rolled up from her toes to her head. The look in his eyes, those large black pupils reminding her of an eagle on the hunt, made her feel like quarry beneath his intense gaze. It wasn't a threatening feeling, either. What was it?

Colt removed his hat and held it in his hand. "Are you the woman I'm supposed to meet?" he asked, wariness in his tone. He hoped she was, especially given she was far more beautiful in person.

"I am," she said. Holding out her hand, she said, "I'm Shelly Godwin."

Taking her soft, warm hand into his, he murmured, "Colt Black. It's nice to meet you, Shelly." He released her hand. "I don't know about you, but this has been a crazy few weeks. I have dreams all the time, but this is the first one that told me to meet someone at a specific place and time. Frankly, I didn't think it was real." Now, he was glad it had been. His heart sang with joy, as much as he tried to suppress it. She seemed to have no place in his realm where he battled evil on a daily basis.

Nervously, Shelly touched her cheek. "I didn't trust my dreams completely, either. But here you are!" It was impossible to not be drawn to this quiet, intensely powerful cowboy. He was easily six feet tall, lanky and had a tense, even dangerous energy surrounding him. Shelly felt completely out of her league with this man. And clearly, he was a man's man. Not like the boy-men she'd had in her life. "Where do dreams begin and end?" she asked rhetorically, stepping away. He was too close. Too overwhelming to her interested feminine senses.

Shrugging, Colt settled his hat back on his head. "I don't really know, Ms. Godwin. I'm a stranger to this kind of thing, too. I feel like I'm in a mystery and I have some puzzle pieces, but I don't know what it all means. Or how they fit together." He gave her an intense look. "I have information for you. I think it might explain what we're doing here. If we share what we know, we might be able to understand it."

Chapter 3

Shelly said, "Come on, let's sit down on this bench over here beneath the fir tree." That sense of danger, of hyperalertness, swirled around him. Colt Black looked around, his brows drawn downward. What was he looking for? she wondered. Shelly opened herself up to feel whatever it was but nothing seemed out of the ordinary.

Nodding, Colt walked with her. It was impossible to ignore her graceful carriage, the way Shelly held her head. The look in her hazel eyes mesmerized him. More than anything, Colt liked the blanket of freckles across her nose and cheeks. She seemed part excited child molded with the sensible maturity of a young woman.

The warm breeze brought the scent of pine to him once again as he sat at a respectful distance from her on the iron bench. Taking off his hat, he turned to her. She leaned back, hands in her lap. Colt launched into his dreams and shared them with her. She sat listening intently. When he was done, he shared with him what she knew from her two dreams.

"What I can surmise," Shelly told him after relaying her dreams, "is that an emerald sphere is somewhere in this park. I saw two rocks, one white and one black. Each is scored down the center and a small vortex whirls between them. The emerald sphere is there."

Colt nodded. "I'm familiar with vortexes. I've never seen a round emerald, though." He was powerfully drawn to her and tried to rein in his feelings. Under no circumstances could he act upon his physical desire. No woman was safe around him for long.

"I wrote a book on vortexes and I've been trained from childhood to find them. But more important is finding that sphere before this unknown sorcerer does. My dream didn't say who the sorcerer was. Frankly, I've never had any interface with them." A murkiness came to his blue eyes. Again, he looked around, as if searching for something. Shelly almost asked what, but decided that would be rude.

A chill worked up Colt's spine at the word *sorcerer*. His mouth tightened. He didn't tell her about Yellow Teeth. Whatever his fears, he knew he had to keep them to himself to help find this mysterious sphere. "You didn't see the sorcerer in your dream?"

"No." With a frustrated sigh, Shelly said, "Who or what he is, I don't know. I only know he could kill us. I've never been on this kind of life-and-death mission, Colt. Have you?"

He held her inquiring hazel gaze. "Yes." The word came out abruptly.

"Oh." Shivering internally, Shelly felt more than saw an energy radiating outward from his aura. It was dark red, which could mean fear, anger or strength. His blue eyes were unreadable, his face suddenly tense. And yet, she felt drawn to this man who had walls as thick as Fort Knox surrounding him. Shelly couldn't translate the malignant sense of danger around him.

"Do you have the ability to feel a sorcerer around?" she asked. "Because my training is not in that area at all."

Colt tried to force himself to relax. "I do. I'm a medicine man in training for my people and we're taught to recognize evil in all forms whether it's physical or in spirit."

"That's good to know. All I can feel is if I like or

don't like someone. I get a feeling—" and she touched her head "—here. Like a red flag warning."

"You see auras?"

"Yes. You, too?"

"Yes," he told her. Why, oh, why did she have to have that innocent look his sister Mary had had? Colt felt his heart contract with anguish.

"I have no direct experience with sorcery. All I know is how to find a vortex." Shelly smiled warmly. "I think you're going to have to be the guard dog on this mission."

"I'll try," he said. Colt allowed himself to absorb the pleasure of her sunlight energy. "I'll do everything I can to keep us safe while we look for the sphere." A sense of fierce protectiveness welled up in Colt. Above all, he wanted to keep Shelly away from the Skin Walker. Even now, as he looked around, Colt felt the stalking energy of Yellow Teeth. There were thousands of trees around and the spirit of the evil witch could be hiding behind any one of them watching. Watching and waiting for an opportunity.

Shelly reached out and touched his bare arm. The muscles leaped beneath her fingertips. "You're a warrior at heart, Colt. I can see it in your aura and in your eyes." She didn't add that he wore armor and that she felt that sense of combat-readiness just a heartbeat away. All of it made him dangerous and provocative to her. She wondered why he hid so much from her. Why he was walled up and untouchable. That was it. *Untouchable.* Maybe that would be best, Shelly decided. Just because she was drawn to Colt didn't mean he was any good in a relationship. Hadn't she learned her lesson yet? Look, but don't touch?

"I'm not a warrior," he snapped. Not after allowing Mary to be kidnapped. A true warrior would have stopped it. Would have rescued her. But he'd done none of those things.

"All right, then you're a gallant knight," Shelly insisted, stung by his unexpected retort. She released her hand from his arm, figuring he probably didn't want to be touched. His skin was copper-smooth, hard-muscled, and she could tell he worked outside for a living. It would be tough for her to stay businesslike with him since he was so painfully attractive.

"I don't see myself like a gallant knight," he said, glaring at her.

"Fair enough. Let's treat this mission seriously. I have no idea if we can find the sphere or what to do with it. Do you?"

Colt shook his head. "Not a clue. If this is a sacred object, the spirit, once we find it, may tell us what to do next."

"I hope you're right." Looking around, she tried

to relax against the bench. There was such an invisible, explosive quality to this man. "This is such a beautiful place." Maybe a little chitchat would ease the tension between them.

Colt saw a strand of red hair dip across her temple and she pushed it back behind her delicate ear. He felt like a starving wolf. His naked desire for Shelly shocked him. For whatever reason, his need of a woman had turned up in volume and he found himself hungry for her. It was a guilty pleasure and Colt wasn't going to deny it, but she was off-limits to him.

And then, a bone-chillingly cold energy struck Colt. Instantly, he sat up, eyes narrowed. He *knew* that feeling! *Yellow Teeth.* And he was nearby. *Damn!* Standing suddenly, hands resting tensely on hips, he noticed Shelly giving him a questioning look, puzzlement in her hazel eyes. Where was the Skin Walker? Inwardly, Colt felt his stomach knot. At the same time, an old anger simmered deep within him, a killing anger. He wanted to kill Yellow Teeth in spirit. Oh, his father had killed his physical body, but Colt knew in spirit, the Skin Walker was even more dangerous than before. If he didn't stay on guard, the Skin Walker would possess his body and cut the silver cord to it and he'd die. And then Yellow Teeth would have Colt's body to walk around in. One day, Colt knew, the witch spirit would stop circling him and finally confront him in one last battle. Only one of them would win.

"What is it?" Shelly asked, concerned as she stood up. She had felt Colt go on guard. The power of his response physically buffeted her and showed her just how strong his energy was. Gulping, she tried to read his face as he scanned their surroundings for some unseen enemy. "What are you sensing?" she finally asked, sitting on the edge of the bench.

"Nothing," he said. "It's nothing." No sense in scaring her. Shelly had no training in the dark side and was completely at risk because of it. Only he stood between the dark side and her.

Rebuffed, Shelly wondered what she'd gotten herself into. Clearly, there was danger. She could sense it without seeing it. And Colt knew there was danger, too. His hands slid off his hips and hung tensely at his sides as he slowly moved around and looked at everyone on the sidewalk that passed them. Who was he looking for? Who else knew they were here?

YELLOW TEETH SMILED with anticipation. He stopped at the male assistant's desk outside the *Tupay*'s Dark Lord's office.

"You can go in now," the male assistant told him mentally.

With a brusque nod, Yellow Teeth opened the door and stepped into Victor Carancho Guerra's office in the *Tupay* castle. As a Skin Walker and a trained witch in the dark arts, he was one of Victor's many soldiers who lived in spirit but worked on the earth plane. He came to the safety of the *Tupay* fortress for training. Because of his powers, Yellow Teeth was in the advanced paranormal training classes. Today, though, something had happened and he wanted to take it directly to the Dark Lord himself.

Entering, Yellow Teeth saw the man who ran the *Tupay* empire. He was lean with long black hair streaked with silver, a goatee, a white face set with flat, lifeless black eyes. Yellow Teeth had never approached this powerful being before. Bowing with respect, he said, "My lord, I come to you because I interrupted a dream by a *Taqe* that you may find of interest."

"Sit," Victor said, gesturing to a wooden chair in front of his desk. The assistant quietly shut the door.

"My lord, I had heard of you being able to steal one of the emerald spheres earlier from the *Taqe*."

"Yes. So?" Victor stared at the tall Navajo man in spirit. He knew Yellow Teeth was one of his soldiers he'd ordered back to the Navajo reservation to hunt *Taqe*. Yellow Teeth had earned his name: tall and pathetically thin, his face narrow with high cheekbones and eyes of a lifeless brown color, when Yellow Teeth opened his mouth the canine teeth in the spirit's mouth were far longer than usual. And because they were long, the Navajo Skin Walker could not quite close his mouth. Drool and bubbles foamed at the corners of his mouth as a result.

"My lord, I was near a *Taqe*'s hogan a week ago. I was stalking him. I lay in wait outside the wall of his hogan and stole into his dream while he was asleep."

"You're sure he's *Taqe?*" Victor asked, frowning. He leaned back in his chair, hands folded across his belly. Yellow Teeth had long black-and-gray hair. In earth years he was about fifty, his face deeply lined and copper-colored.

"Yes, my lord. He wears the two entwined circles on the back of his neck. You had assigned us to kill anyone on my reservation who had that symbol."

"Quite right. That's the Vesica Pisces symbol that tells us he is a Warrior for the Light. Your job is to take care of that particular reservation. Right now—" Victor looked through some stats he had on hand "—there are twenty-five Skin Walkers either in human or spirit form down there who routinely hunt for them among your nation."

Yellow Teeth smiled a little. "That is so, my lord. I have killed five *Taqe* so far." He waved his hand with its long dirty fingernails. "I had caught and killed this man's sister many years ago. She, too, had the symbol on the back of her neck. And then their father stalked me and killed me with a rifle." He shrugged. "After passing over, I came here and was trained and went back to continue my work down on the reservation from the spirit side."

"And that's why you were stalking this *Taqe?*"

"Yes. I've made it my revenge to kill Colt Black sooner or later."

"He had a dream and you intercepted it?"

Nodding, Yellow Teeth shared the dream. Instantly, he saw the Dark Lord sit up, more than a little interested in the dream's contents.

"Black and this woman have met one another in Banff?" Victor demanded, excited.

"They have, my lord. I just eavesdropped on their conversation with one another from a safe distance. The woman with the red hair carries the Vesica Pisces symbol on the back of her neck, too."

"This is good news, Yellow Teeth," Victor said with a smile. "I was waiting to see where the next sphere might show up. We had worked with the one we managed to steal and it, too, showed that area of Canada. Your dream, however, gives us the details and the identities of the two *Taqe* charged with finding the fifth sphere. Well done!"

Glowing beneath the unexpected praise, Yellow Teeth smiled, his canines fully exposed, the drool inching out of the corners of his mouth. He wiped it away with the back of his hand. "Thank you, my lord. If you are going to go there, I would like to be considered a part of your mission. I know Colt Black. I can be of great help to you. Black knows I'm stalking him and, one day, I will kill him as I killed his sister."

Nodding, Victor smiled a triumphant smile. "Well, keep your revenge at bay. And don't worry, Yellow Teeth, you'll be with the team I'm assembling right now."

VICTOR GUERRA congratulated himself after Yellow Teeth left. By stealing the fourth emerald sphere from the *Taqe* at the Vesica Pisces Foundation, he'd struck gold. After getting the beautifully hand-carved sphere back to the *Tupay* stronghold in the fourth dimension, he'd worked with it until the spirit within sent him knowledge of the place where the next sphere, the fifth one, would be found—Banff National Park in Alberta, Canada. Although the sphere did not give him specific information, he'd been shown four lakes, and, having drawn their shapes, he'd realized it was in the vicinity of Lake Louise. And then, Yellow Teeth had entered and handed him the rest of the information. Victor rubbed his hands with silent glee over this good luck. Certainly, the tide had turned in his favor.

The hard part had been done. Victor had called one of his most trusted knights, Lothar, to accompany him into the third-dimensional world of Earth. And he'd brought an up-and-coming *Tupay* spirit by the name of Jeff Anderson along as an apprentice. Jeff had the intelligence and aptitude Victor needed for his priority missions to Earth. One day, Jeff would become a knight. Of course, Yellow Teeth would be there as counsel and Victor had promised him that after the fifth sphere was found and retrieved, he could kill Colt Black. The Skin Walker had howled with delight.

The spirit of the emerald had shown Victor a rocky lakeshore. There, he'd seen a white rock and a black rock, each scored down the center. What had mystified him was the whirling tornado-like energy that danced between these rocks. Later, after asking Lothar about this phenomenon, Victor had learned it was a planetary energy known as a vortex. Hundreds of thousands of them were placed around the Earth along the spiderweb-like ley-line system that enclosed the planet. The emerald sphere was on a shore with those two rocks and a vortex.

Victor's soldiers had watched Vesica Pisces Foundation's headquarters in Quito, Ecuador, twenty-four hours a day, but there seemed to be no team leaving to hunt for the next sphere. And then, he got it: the sphere had shown him the next location, it had not sent that same information to the *Taqe* foundation. Sitting at his desk, Victor laughed long and loud. The joke was on them! Finally, things had taken a turn for the better. The *Taqe* were probably in high drama over receiving no instructions.

Victor, who had been the Dark Lord of the *Tupay* for a long time, knew better than to rest on his laurels over this realization. It was entirely possible that those in the *Taqe* stronghold, the Village of the Clouds, could find out this information another way. Victor never misjudged *Taqe* inventiveness nor their reach to acquire information. Further, only the *Taqe* were allowed into the Akashic Records, not the *Tupay*. As he rubbed his chin, he wondered if their leaders, Alaria and Adaire, were already looking through the records of time that recorded every soul's thousands of incarnations. They might search there for hints or clues to the location of the sixth sphere.

VICTOR GUERRA LIKED the body of Trip Nelson. He'd possessed the athletic young man an hour earlier. He was blond and blue-eyed, and he worked as a guide at the world-famous Fairmont Château Lake Louise.

Guerra had followed the two *Taqe* that Yellow Teeth had led him to earlier. Victor had watched from a safe distance, assessing the red-haired woman and the black-haired man. Each had the silver in their auras. He couldn't get close because he saw that they both had strong paranormal skills in place. The male had a protective shield, as well. Both had the Vesica Pisces birthmark on the back of their necks. Indeed, as Yellow Teeth had said, they were *Taqe*. If he got close enough to eavesdrop on them, they'd get wary. The real question was, were they highly skilled enough to detect him camouflaged as he was by the human body? After all, his true aura was not visible. The *Taqe* couple would only perceive the aura of the human he had possessed. In Victor's thousands of years of experience, most *Taqe* could not perceive a possession. But he couldn't underestimate their powers. Yellow Teeth had already warned him the male was a powerful medicine man, not to be trifled with.

Victor stood with his hands in the pockets of his brown corduroy pants. Lothar was at his side, along with Jeff. After Lothar had spotted the *Taqe* team, he and Jeff had possessed twin American brothers who were visiting Lake Louise for a week. They were in their twenties, strong and fit.

"Well?" Victor said to Lothar. "What do you think?" He watched as the two *Taqe* got up from the bench and walked toward the hotel.

"My lord," Lothar said, turning to him, "I would counsel patience. Let us follow them and sit in the lobby and just watch and wait. We can press one of the hotel people for details about them later."

Jeff pushed the toe of his hiking boot into the dirt just off the path that wound around one half of Lake Louise. "My lord? I'm in training and I don't know if you want my thoughts on this or not."

Victor looked into Jeff's eyes. They had been smart to choose the bodies of healthy young men. "Of course I want to know what you think." His voice sharpened. "You're in training to do this work on your own someday. The only way to get good is to allow us into your thoughts."

"If we sit in the hotel lobby and they see the three of us, will they know who we really are?" Jeff asked.

"No," Victor said, pleased with his question. "So long as we remain in possessed bodies, ninety-nine percent of the *Taqe* cannot detect us."

"But our auras? Surely they can tell who we are by reading them," he pressed, frowning.

With a shake of his head, Victor said, "No, the aura of the person we've possessed remains intact. Some of the colors of the aura may change or darken. That cannot be helped. Most *Taqe* who read auras are only as good as their experience. And an aura can have a million different combinations of light and dark colors. I am counting on them to not realize who we really are."

"Chances are these *Taqe* will see some darkness

in our auras and think we are either sad, depressed or worried about something," Lothar told the student. "They probably won't pick up on the fact we've taken up residence in these bodies. Until we know for sure, we can't assume. We must remain conservative and not press them too closely."

"All right," Jeff murmured. He rubbed his square chin and enjoyed being back in a physical body. "And so, we stalk by waiting and observing?"

Lothar nodded. "I see exhaustion in Colt Black's aura. He came from Arizona, a long journey. The woman lives in a town about fifty miles away. My guess is they are going to rest for a while."

"Let's go in and observe," Victor said. Yellow Teeth remained in the fourth dimension and at a distance after identifying the couple. Victor did not want to put the male *Taqe* on guard by detecting the witch's presence—not yet.

The men fell into step behind the Dark Lord. The day was sunny and the temperature was a wonderful eighty degrees Fahrenheit. Jeff enjoyed his human body. Never mind that he had stolen it from its owner whose spirit was now squashed inside. This was his first assignment. Since his last incarnation as a U.S. Army Ranger in the Second World War, when he had died on Omaha Beach, he had remained in *Tupay* training school. He was determined to do his best for the Dark Lord.

Inside the hotel, Victor inquired at the busy desk about the *Taqe* couple. Lothar gestured to Jeff to sit down on one of the overstuffed chairs in the spacious lobby. From their vantage point, they could see not only the stairs but the elevators. Victor came over and stood between them.

Keeping his voice low, he said, "I read the clerk's mind. Their names are Colt Black and Shelly Godwin, just as Yellow Teeth told us. They're in rooms 204 and 206. They are tired and went up to rest." Twisting a look toward the elevators, Victor added, "My bet is they will take a nap and then meet down here later for dinner."

Lothar nodded. "That sounds reasonable."

"Which restaurant?" Jeff wondered, looking through the throngs of people moving through the massive hotel. "I think there are three or four restaurants in this place."

Victor shrugged. "It doesn't matter. Jeff, you stay here for two hours and watch. Then Lothar will relieve you. I'm going back to my residence. Trip lives in a building near the hotel. Call me telepathically if you spot them. Follow them discreetly and see which restaurant they choose."

Rubbing his hands, Lothar grinned. "A stake-out." He turned to Jeff. "You get first watch, my boy."

"Of course," Jeff said. He was, after all, the underling here. Lothar was a famous *Tupay* knight. As his bosses left, Jeff settled into the chair. How good it felt!

Jeff's host-body was that of a botanist, which could turn out to be useful if the *Taqe* needed help. He could present himself as a helpful tourist and not rouse their suspicions. Smiling, Jeff watched the nonstop flow of people. Fourteen million people visited this place every year. For Jeff, who had been in spirit since 1944, this was a liberating experience, being among the living. He truly loved drinking coffee, eating real food again and being able to appreciate all those things the third dimension offered.

Watching the children and teens with their families brought an ache to his heart. Jeff knew he was supposed to be immune to such things. Perhaps he just needed more time in spirit. Jeff had never lost his desire to be back in this world. He'd loved being alive. He'd always regretted that a bullet had ripped through him while he climbed a cliff with his squad. As he fell and lay dying, the panic overwhelmed him. Never would he be able to love again, smell a flower, savor his parents' Iowa farm home during Thanksgiving. Small things, but so important to him.

Right after his death, his wife, Janet, had had twin boys. He'd watched them grow up without his presence. His sons went on to marry and now Jeff saw five new grandchildren in his Earth family. The one that he felt closest to was Mary Anderson. She was twenty-eight years old and very metaphysical.

As a quilt designer with a hobby of drawing Middle Ages churches in Europe, she was famous for her designs and artistic renderings. Mary was an introvert—shy, excruciatingly sensitive to the harsh world she lived in. And, like Jeff, she had a strong sense of faith in the unknown. Yes, it was a pleasure to follow the lives of all his family, whether he was with them or not.

Jeff realized that he wasn't fully a *Tupay* yet. Those that had made the transition did not miss Earth, their last family or their five senses as he did. For whatever reason, the Dark Lord himself had chosen him for this assignment and Jeff was grateful. Above all, he'd never let his bosses know how much he liked coming back here. If they found out, he'd be booted off the mission schooling assignments for good. No, best to keep his secret exactly that.

Jeff's brows rose as he saw a couple come out of one of the elevators. It was them! Excited, he sat up. Then he remembered to remain slouched and seemingly oblivious. The woman wore jeans, a white short-sleeved blouse and a straw hat to shade her face. She had on hiking boots and carried a red day pack. Her partner wore similar clothing except his was a long-sleeved white shirt with the cuffs rolled up to just below his elbows. Where were they going? The clerk had said they'd gone up to rest. Had they changed their minds?

Sitting up, sweaty from fear of being discovered, Jeff did not make eye contact with the *Taqe*. They passed within five feet of him, and he was thrilled that they didn't seem to notice his aura or its colors. Jeff waited until they'd passed him. As they got to the revolving doors that would lead out into the beautiful summer day, he stood up. He pulled the cell phone out of the pocket of his jeans and quickly dialed as he walked to the doors. Lucky for him, Lothar had introduced him to the twenty-first-century gadget. As he walked outside into the sunshine, he stopped. *How stupid.* He didn't need to call the Dark Lord on a cell phone! All he had to do was send him a mental message. Being in body again in a different era caused him confusion, though it was understandable. Moving off to one side of the entrance, he focused his mental energies as he'd been taught at *Tupay* school and sent the Dark Lord his information.

Chapter 4

"This is a gorgeous lake," Shelly remarked as they stood on the flat dirt path at the shore. The waters were more emerald than turquoise because of the slant of the afternoon sun. Breathing it all in, she sighed. "I love the smell of pine trees. Don't you?"

Nodding, Colt didn't feel so nostalgic. He felt on edge for no discernible reason. Maybe he was tired, and knowing that Yellow Teeth's spirit had arrived earlier compounded his exhaustion. Shelly seemed completely at ease, her hazel eyes shining with excitement. They stood off to one side of the path as groups of people ambled by. "Did you feel anything odd in the lobby?" Colt asked.

Shelly glanced back toward the hotel. "No. Why, did you?"

Colt grimaced. "I'm not sure. I'm tired and when I'm down like this, I can't access what I sense very easily."

"Oh, that." She slid her fingers beneath the nylon straps of her day pack. "I'm like you—too tired to be on." Trying to talk with Colt was like getting a stubborn mule to move. He seemed just as tense as before. Talkative, he was not.

"That's what I thought. Maybe we should just snoop around but not do any serious exploring today. Get a good night's sleep before we start this grand adventure?" he suggested in a clipped tone. He noticed his gruff tone hurt her, and every emotion registered on her expressive face. If she only knew just how much he secretly wanted her—in his arms and in his bed. This mission was the last thing he needed, especially with Yellow Teeth breathing down his neck. Being with Shelly, soaking up her lively, bubbly energy, made it bearable. He just didn't want to cause her pain.

As Shelly watched him deal with some internal struggle, she felt the soft breeze graze her face. The sunlight dappled like gold coins across the lake. The breeze created ripples here and there across the emerald surface. Surrounding the lake were snow-clad mountains with a cobalt sky above them. Truly, this was a magical place. It always had been for her as a child when she'd come here often with her parents. Shelly had never lost her awestruck feeling about Lake Louise. But now, seeing the worry in Colt's blue eyes, she forced herself to pay attention. It was far too easy to be taken captive by the raw landscape of the Canadian Rockies.

"It's hard to stay focused when you have this kind of beauty surrounding you." Shelly gestured to the lake and the magnificent granite Rockies swathed in snow at the higher altitudes. "Look at this. I never get tired of coming here just to sit and enjoy it."

"It's like Flagstaff, Arizona, in some ways," Colt said. The nonstop laughter and talking from the tourists were making him edgy. He was used to silence. Just the wind, the birds and the howl of an occasional coyote around him. Taking Shelly by the upper arm, Colt guided her off the path until they stood next to the pebbly lakeshore. Some of the discordant and disruptive noise floated away from them. He forced himself to drop his hand from her elbow.

"It's all the noise, isn't it?" Shelly asked, giving him an understanding look. Her elbow tingled wildly in the wake of his rough touch. It had been unexpected. For a moment, that facade melted and surprise flared in his eyes.

"How did you know?"

A warmth cascaded through Shelly. She felt like cheering. At last, she'd glimpsed the real Colt Black beneath that heavy, protective armor he wore. "I'm the same. I think all sensitive people become raw over nonstop talking." She smiled softly. "Most of the places I go to find vortexes are out in the country, although they are found in cities and suburbs, too. I love hiking the trails of the countryside. I have birds who sing to me."

"We're more alike than I thought," Colt said, a little stunned by her admittance. Shelly had the disconcerting ability to throw him off stride. But then, Colt reminded himself, she was not a Navajo from the reservation. Those who lived outside the res had an entirely different way of communicating with one another. It was actions, not words, that were important to Colt.

"You think you're the only one who loves peace and quiet?" She chuckled and smiled up into his hooded blue eyes. For a moment, Shelly felt as if he were going to sweep her into his arms and kiss her. *What a thought!* Yet, when her gaze settled on his very male mouth, a host of riffling sensations were triggered from her throat down to her lower body. Colt would be a wonderful kisser. Yet, with the heavy armor surrounding him she wondered if he let anyone get too close. Why did it matter to her? Chastising herself over her feminine curiosity, Shelly realized how powerfully she was drawn to this intense, quiet man.

"Excuse me!" a voice hailed them from the trail above.

A frisson of warning shot through Colt over the man's loud intrusive voice. Whirling around, he stared up at a young man who had a guide badge on his shirt, along with his name, Trip Nelson. The guide gave them a toothy, welcoming smile as he made his way down to the lakefront where they stood.

"Hello. I'm Trip Nelson, a guide from the hotel. You two look ready to hike. Can I possibly be of help?"

Colt opened his mouth to say no.

"Sure," Shelly invited.

Giving her a warning look, Colt felt the hair on his neck rise in warning as the tall, robust youth joined them. Despite the man's gaiety and big smile, Colt saw flat and lifeless eyes. This was just the beginning of their troubles. Colt stepped forward to keep the guide from coming any closer. His stomach churned and knotted as he stared into the man's eyes. Something was terribly wrong here. But what? Colt had never encountered this sensation before.

"We're just fine by ourselves," Colt said in a snarl, standing between the man and Shelly. He visualized white light in the form of a huge, thick bubble around himself and her. And as he did this, Trip's brows rose in surprise. Did the guide feel the protective action?

Shelly frowned. She couldn't understand Colt moving in front of her. Peeking around him, she said, "That's not true. Trip?"

"Yes, ma'am," he murmured, giving her a slight bow of deference.

Shelly tried to navigate her partner's moods, all while entreating the help of this perfectly friendly guide. Trip's hair was short and straight. He held a green canvas hat in his left hand. Everything about him shouted that he was a rugged outdoors type. His skin was deeply tanned and she liked the apparently ever-present smile on his wide mouth. "We're looking for trails around Lake Louise."

Victor laughed silently as he stood next to Shelly. Neither *Taqe* sensed the possession. That was good. The red-haired woman didn't have a clue. The thrill of the hunt made Victor giddy. However, her partner, the strong silent type, glared at him with a level of threat that made him wary. Victor could see the combativeness in Black's aura. Since his walls were in place, Victor knew Black could not access his thoughts to find out his identity. "Well, I can help with that." He pulled a map from his back pocket and quickly opened it up before them.

This would give Victor a valuable chance to assess them. Shelly seemed curious but absolutely stupid. Black, on the other hand, was tense and didn't trust him at all even if he didn't know why. Opening the map fully, Victor had them hold the corners so that it was open between them.

"What type of trails are you looking for?" Trip asked with enthusiasm.

"I want to know if there's a trail all the way around Lake Louise," Colt said. He didn't like Trip. Alarms were going off inside him. The bubble of protection would hold for another thirty minutes. It frustrated Colt that he didn't understand what the hell he was picking up on. He kept giving Shelly looks, but she seemed completely unaffected by this guide's strange aura.

"No, sir, there isn't. You have this wide path which is a trail that starts here at the hotel and goes to the northeast part of the lake. Then, there's a second trail on the other side of the lake." He gave them a warm smile. "Why do you want to hike around all of the lake?"

"Because we want to," Colt growled.

Shelly frowned at Colt's tone. He was clearly uncomfortable. Why? She didn't know, but she trusted his instincts. She decided to lie. "I'm a photographer of wildflowers, Trip. The lakes up here are pretty much free of brush on the shore and it makes it easy for me to walk and hunt." Shelly wanted Nelson to assume they were just a couple of tourists on holiday.

"Ah, I see," Trip murmured with geniality. "Well, you're right. These are glacier lakes and when the Ice Age came through here ten thousand years ago, all the lakes were changed. As the ice melted, millions of stones that had been ground up were dropped in this region." He gestured toward the bank. "There's little sand and hardly any soil around the lakes. Just enough to encourage grass, bushes or trees to thrive near the banks without barring your way to the shore. You'll find some wildflowers as a result."

"So, it should be pretty easy to walk around the opposite part of the lake on this side?" Colt asked.

"Well—"

"We can rent a canoe, Colt. That will be the easier thing to do."

"Good idea!" Trip smiled and pointed toward the marina down about a quarter of a mile. "You can rent a canoe by the hour. It won't be difficult to paddle into this area—" and he tapped the map with his index finger "—and look for flowers along the shore. Besides, the canoe can carry all your photo equipment. It's an easy way to scour the shoreline."

"Great, that's what we'll do," Shelly said, smiling fully.

Trip folded up the map. "Is there anything else I can do for you?" Black glared at him with such venom that Victor decided he'd had enough for the day. The Navajo medicine man had one hand balled into a fist at his side. Victor didn't want to start a fight. Clearly, Black was picking up something or he wouldn't be so damned threatening. *Best to leave.*

"You can go," Colt said with authority. Of all the people Trip Nelson could have zeroed in on, he wondered, why them? There were hundreds of people walking up and down the sidewalk around the lakeshore. Why had he chosen them? Colt gave Trip an intense look and opened himself up more than he should. By opening up, Colt could assess a person's aura far better, but it left him vulnerable. Reminding himself he had the white-light protection, Colt risked it.

Shelly gave Trip a smile. "Thanks for all your great info, Trip. We've got to get going."

Victor grunted inwardly. This Indian was actually probing his aura! He could feel the fingerlike projections poking into the energy layers around him. Under normal circumstances, Victor would kill a person who tried this on him, but he couldn't now. He needed to escape from Black. Trip scrambled lithely up the rocky slope. "Well, if there is anything else, I'm always here. My job is to help our hotel guests get the most out of their visit."

Victor turned away. His mind was spinning with questions. He glanced back to see the Navajo medicine man glaring at him, his mouth set. This was one dangerous *Taqe*. The double ring birthmark on his neck meant he was a Warrior for the Light. Victor heaved a sigh of relief. While it was true he had more power than Black, this was neither the time nor place to unveil it. He needed these two to help find the next sphere.

Walking quickly toward the hotel, Victor wondered why the pair would want to circumnavigate the entire coastline of Lake Louise. Were those two boulders located around here? He slowed and turned on the other side of the path, hidden by groups of tourists. The *Taqe* were walking toward the marina. Scratching his head, Victor figured the emerald sphere was closer than he thought. What did the *Taqe* know that he didn't?

Ordinarily, he could dig into anyone's mind and telepathically root through the contents without a problem. However, Black had thrown up a defensive perimeter. Of all the bad luck—this guy was a superb warrior. That complicated things a great deal.

Lothar and Jeff joined him.

"Anything, my lord?" Lothar demanded.

With a shake of his head, Victor told them what

had transpired. When he mentioned Black's power and defensiveness, both men's brows rose in surprise.

"That's a bad sign," Lothar said, unhappy. "The Vesica Pisces Foundation is sending in their best soldiers."

Snorting, Victor grimaced. "Warriors are testy. And Black was this close—" he held up his thumb and index finger "—to hitting me. He knew something was very wrong with Trip Nelson."

"Do you think he figured it out?" Jeff asked.

Shaking his head, Victor muttered, "No, but I can't go up to him again or he may put it together. We can't risk that."

"Poking into your aura must have felt uncomfortable," Lothar said.

"Not exactly fun," Victor agreed. "The fact he'd even do it tells me he's fearless in the face of danger."

"Is it possible that he was trying to goad you into a fight to see who you really were?" Jeff wondered.

"Possibly," Victor said.

Lothar gave the student a warning look. "You never do that to someone else's aura. That's assault, pure and simple."

"Do you think Black knew your aura was beneath that outer one, my lord?" Jeff asked.

"Who knows?" Victor growled. "He caught me

off guard with that maneuver. But there was little I could do about it except get the hell out of there."

"If you'd allowed him, would he have found your real aura by poking around like that?" Jeff wondered.

"Absolutely," Lothar said. "It would be a dead giveaway if he had broken through the fields of that first aura."

"Yes," Victor muttered, "and wouldn't he have been surprised to find me hidden in there?"

They all chuckled and nodded.

"Perhaps the sphere is hidden where there is a patch of wildflowers?" Lothar wondered.

"That doesn't make sense. It's a cover. I could see the telltale colors of a lie in her aura."

Jeff looked at the two older spirits. He gazed at the turquoise lake. "Is it possible the sphere is in the water near the shore?"

"Anything is possible," Victor said.

"Then all we can do is follow them," Jeff said.

Lothar tapped a pair of binoculars hung around his neck. "We will—from a distance. Let's hope they do their hiking in the daylight and sleep at night. Makes it easier on us."

Victor cursed softly and continued to watch the pair. Eventually, they disappeared into the crowds along the walk. Turning, he said, "Lothar, Jeff, go rent a canoe. Keep close enough to them without rousing suspicion. Watch what they do and where they go."

Jeff wanted to rub his hands together in joy but refrained. He had been an Iowa farm boy growing up in the 1920s and 1930s. His parents had owned a huge grain farm near a lake. He'd had a canoe, and, during the spring and summer, he'd fished all the time. This mission was turning out to be wonderful in so many ways for him.

"Jeff?" Lothar snapped. "Where's your head, boy? Come on!"

Caught red-handed, Jeff saw Victor's flat, black eyes narrow upon him. "Coming," he called.

"Stay alert!" Victor snarled at the young *Tupay*.

Jeff leaped toward Lothar, stung by the Dark Lord's warning. How anyone could remain immune to the beauty of this world was beyond him. He thought about his family and wished he had time to peek in on how they were doing. It was his favorite thing to do on a given day at the *Tupay* fortress. With this mission, it was impossible to check in. His granddaughter, Mary Anderson, the one who was an artist and quilt designer, was going on a trip to Edinburgh, Scotland. She had been hired by the town to give a series of workshops on her famous quilt designs. Hurrying, he caught up with Lothar and grinned.

"I can hardly wait to climb into a canoe."

Scowling, Lothar said, "You're like an excitable puppy. Calm down, will you?"

How could he? Jeff saw this as fun, not work. He would savor the canoe trip. The water was smooth out there, a slight breeze and warm sunlight embracing him. Right now, he felt as though he'd walked into heaven.

Chapter 5

"Why didn't you like Trip Nelson?" Shelly walked at Colt's side as they moved toward the canoe-rental wharf. People flowed around them on the warm, beautiful afternoon. Jays shrieked in trees near the sidewalk, looking for handouts from the tourists. Squirrels and chipmunks also kept an eager watch from the sides of the path.

Colt cut her a glance. Shelly seemed so damned innocent in his dark world. "I got a red flag on him." He rubbed the back of his neck. "My hair stood up on end. Any time that happens, it signals danger to me."

"Did you see his aura? It looked okay to me." She enjoyed his nearness. Colt was tall, lean and walked with a fluid grace. Even more palpable was her womanly desire for him. He was mysterious and unapproachable. Worse, he was utterly masculine and dangerous in a sensual kind of way. She couldn't stop looking at his mouth. Usually, it was pursed, the corners drawn in. When he relaxed, it was a mouth worth kissing. And kissing again. Where was all of this heat coming from? Frustrated with herself, she tried to ignore that aspect of him, but it was proving impossible.

"There was murkiness in his astral field. You didn't see that?" Inwardly, Colt kicked himself. His gaze drifted from her widened eyes down to that wide, soft mouth of hers. Did she know how tempting she really was to him?

Shelly shrugged. "I agree, it was murky, but nothing too unusual."

Colt noticed the slight shadows beneath her eyes and added, "Why don't we go down to rent a canoe for tomorrow afternoon?" No sense in pursuing this line of talk.

"I like that plan," Shelly said. She knew so little about Colt and she had so many questions. A crazy dream had brought them together: two strangers from two very different worlds. Yet she felt an inexplicable hunger for him. He was composed of incredibly powerful energy. No question he was a warrior, and his cowboy clothes only emphasized his rugged face and nature. All were appealing to her as a woman.

Colt cupped her elbow and steered her through the people to the booth on the bank next to the canoe-docking facility. "Let's do that." He didn't ignore his flesh tingling as he made contact with Shelly. For an instant, Colt saw desire clearly written in her wide hazel eyes. Was she attached? There was no wedding ring on her finger. Not that this was at all relevant to their assignment. He needed to find out more about her.

Her skin tingled pleasantly to his grazing, guiding touch. Shelly wanted excuses just to touch Colt. At the rental booth, he dropped his hand. In no time, they had a red canoe rented for 3:00 p.m. tomorrow. Ticket in hand, he walked her out onto the wide wooden wharf. Colorful canoes were tied to either side of the one-hundred-foot-long area. To Shelly, they reminded her of a rainbow. She wished she had brought her camera. Her Nikon D3 was back in her room, but she promised herself to bring it along with her tomorrow.

As they stood at the end of the dock appreciating the colors of Lake Louise, the tourists out paddling around in rented canoes, Shelly picked up their earlier conversation. "When I saw darkness or dirty colors in his astral field, I thought Trip was probably upset about something."

Shrugging, Colt enjoyed the sunlit warmth on his body. The wind was light and playful. Best of all, Shelly was standing next to him. He liked the way the breeze lifted strands of her hair. There were many colors among the threads with the sunlight dancing across her hair. He wanted to slide his fingers through those strands of gold shimmering with copper and burgundy highlights. She was incredibly beautiful and his heart opened to her. Though, for now, he forced himself to address her statement. "In my experience, the astral body field is changing from minute to minute depending upon what we're feeling at that time."

"How do you know all these things?" Shelly finally asked. She watched a family of four, the mother in the bow and the father at the stern, paddling a green canoe toward them. The two children, both towheads and probably around six and seven, were happily splashing their hands into the lake water. "That was the only fly in the ointment I could see in Trip Nelson's aura, Colt. I figured he was scared of something. The brownish-red color around his solar plexus tells me he feared something. Maybe us?" She glanced up at him. His beautifully shaped mouth was pursed, his brows drawn down as he considered her remarks.

"I'm a medicine man of the Navajo nation," he said abruptly. "My father taught me how to read auras from the time I was a child. When Nelson walked up to us, his field showed fear. You always look for what is out of place."

A medicine man. Well, that answered why Colt was incredibly clairvoyant and could see auras. "You were pretty abrupt with him, but not threatening enough to cause the kind of darkness I saw in his astral field," she countered.

"I was abrupt because the hair on the back of my neck stood up." He almost added, *And if you don't pay attention to subtle warnings like that, you can get killed.* Obviously, they lived in different worlds.

"I wonder if he's been possessed," Shelly murmured.

Colt held her upturned, searching stare. Her red lashes framed her wide, hazel eyes. The pupils were large and black. He felt as if he could fall into her gaze and happily drown, a fulfilled man. Tearing his thoughts away from the personal, he said, "Skin Walkers possess people in my culture. They're men who practice witchcraft and are shape-shifters. They turn themselves into coyotes and then hunt for some unsuspecting Navajo who made the mistake of being out after dark. And once the humans are possessed, they are dead after the Skin Walker is done with them."

"Oh…" Shelly said, feeling a coldness within her. "That sounds…awful.…"

"It is," Colt said. "The Navajo taken over by the Skin Walker is still inside his body, but the witch is in control of him or her. And when the Skin Walker is done with them, he leaves their body and cuts the silver cord. Their spirit is released and the person dies. It's not pretty."

Shelly gulped. "I—I've never seen anything like that happen. I feel like a neophyte around you, Colt. I'm just not into sorcery or evil." And suddenly, Shelly was glad the grim-looking cowboy was on this mission with her. He didn't look like a medicine man, but rather, a wrangler who might work at one of the dude ranches outside Banff.

"The problem is your dream told you there was danger, a sorcerer. In my culture that equates to a witch who creates spells and curses or a witch who can shape-shift into a Skin Walker," Colt said, frustrated. "I don't know how to read Nelson. If a Skin Walker had him, I'd know it in an instant. But this is a different energy and I don't understand what I was sensing. All we can do is watch, listen to our feelings and keep this guy away from us as we search the shore of this lake."

Shelly was sobered by Colt's knowledge…and profoundly shaken. "My gut tells me that wherever these two boulders are you'll find a vortex. Did your father teach you about vortexes, too?"

"We don't call them vortexes. For us, they are simply areas of energy."

There were many benches on either side of the thirty-foot-wide wharf. Impulsively, Shelly slid her hand into his. It was strong, warm, callused from hard work. She looked up, saw the surprise and then desire in his eyes. Again, a sense of danger surrounded her. It was a risk worth taking. Shelly drew him to the last bench. "Come and sit down with me for a moment." She pleaded with him when he hesitated. Clearly, he wanted her and the feeling was mutual. There was a lot to be scared of, but she couldn't help but be excited.

Just getting to touch Shelly was a pleasure for Colt and he gently squeezed her fingers in return. If she were married, she wouldn't have touched him. And the warmth, the invitation, was in her eyes, too. As they sat down close to one another, Colt reluctantly released her hand. If he didn't, well, he'd turn and kiss her senseless. His alertness would be dulled, just in time for Yellow Teeth to strike. Skin Walkers were good at catching their prey off guard.

"Okay," he said, getting back to business. "We need to understand one another's psychic abilities. What strengths and weakness do we have?"

"All right," Shelly said, moving away from him,

to the other end of the bench. Colt was too close, too raw and natural for her to keep her hands in her lap for long. "Here we are, two strangers who have come together because of mutual dreams. I know so little about you."

"I was born on the Navajo reservation. I've lived there my entire life. My father has trained me to be a medicine man like himself. Healing runs in our family."

"You have a wife and kids?"

Pursing his lips, he said, "No, I'm not married. What about you?" There, the question was out.

"No. I'm single and unattached. I live just outside the park in Canmore." She frowned for a moment. "I'm a writer. I wrote a book on vortexes. That's my claim to fame. Normally, I'm on the road, traveling around the world giving workshops on how to find a vortex and what to do with it once you do find one."

As Colt took in this new information, he continued to look around. He sensed Yellow Teeth just on the edges of his periphery, but he didn't want to scare Shelly or show her just how distracted she was. "You're Canadian?" he asked.

"Yes." She saw him digesting the information. And then, Colt was once more looking around. "I feel you so on guard. What's the matter?" Her voice went off pitch. "Are we in danger?"

"There's a Skin Walker named Yellow Teeth who would very much like to possess and kill me," Colt told her. He saw Shelly's eyes go wide and her lips part. Then she caught herself and tried to be all right with the information, but Colt knew it had shocked her.

"A vendetta? Revenge? Is that why he wants to kill you?" Her heart pounded momentarily. Colt was a vital man, a man of nature and hard work. There was nothing lame or weak about him. Shelly couldn't envision Colt being overpowered, much less killed by a Navajo witch.

"Something like that," he said. "I feel him around. I always know how close or far away he is from me." Colt decided not to tell Shelly the rest of the terrible story, about the loss of his sister. He didn't know her that well. It was a wound that would never fully heal until he confronted the Skin Walker and killed him.

Shivering, Shelly said, "That's awful! I don't know if I could live with that kind of knowledge. To be stalked day and night, a witch just waiting to jump inside my body and kick me out…"

"He's after me, not you."

The hardness of his words didn't make Shelly feel any better. Without thinking, she reached out and touched his arm. "That wasn't what I meant, Colt." The moment her fingers touched his flesh, his eyes flickered with desire—for her. Was she crazy? Shelly no longer trusted herself or the signals men gave to her. In the past, she'd completely misread them. Instantly, she lifted her fingertips off his arm. The muscles leaped where she'd grazed his skin.

"You said a Skin Walker is a coyote?" she asked, gulping.

Nodding, Colt tried to ignore the ripple of energy her touch had created up and down his arm. "Yes. They come out at dusk and stalk the reservation until dawn. They can't handle sunlight. They hide and wait and plot during the daylight hours."

"So, we're safe during the day?"

"No."

Tilting her head, she gave him a questioning look.

"Yellow Teeth is in spirit. My father killed him years ago. When a Skin Walker's in spirit, he can come at you day or night."

Real fear ate at Shelly. "That's awful. You've suffered a lot of trauma," she said.

Her ability to empathize touched Colt's heart as nothing had in a long time. Who was this woman? Gazing into her glistening eyes filled with compassion, he found only innocence and trust. The blanket of freckles across her cheeks and nose made her look more like a teenager than the young woman she really was. It brought out Colt's protectiveness. "Yes, my family has suffered greatly because of Yellow Teeth."

Shelly sighed. "I wonder if my dream about the sorcerer is really about Yellow Teeth?"

"I would think it was, but it was your dream. You tell me."

Pushing some strands of hair away from her brow, Shelly shrugged. "This is all new to me. I get prophetic dreams, but nothing like this one. Frankly, I'm surprised you're sitting here with me. I doubted the dream from the beginning. I really didn't think I'd meet anyone here in the park today."

"Me either." For the first time, a hint of a smile curved the corners of his mouth. "I'm used to dealing with the Other Side, but this is a new one to me, too."

"Do you think that Yellow Teeth sent us the dreams?"

Colt digested her question. "I didn't think he could do something like that. I have a lot of barriers up that he can't breach." Looking over at her thoughtful expression, he said, "Maybe he got to you. But that wouldn't make sense. No, I think someone else sent us these twin dreams."

"But who?" She opened her hands, exasperation in her voice. "Are we being guided by someone evil, Colt? Right now, I'm really scared. Vortex work can be dangerous upon occasion, but nothing like this. And I'm really out of my element."

Without thinking, Colt moved his hand to her

slumped shoulder. When his fingers met the soft fabric and he felt the warmth of her flesh beneath it, something happened. The doors of his heart flew open. It caught him off guard. For so long, Colt had resisted women on an emotional level. Oh, he'd had his fair share of liaisons with women, but nothing permanent. He didn't want Yellow Teeth to kill the woman he loved. And as he connected with Shelly, Colt felt all his resolve melt away. There was something so clean and untouched about Shelly that he had no defense against it—or her.

"Don't be afraid," he coaxed in a low voice. His fingers brushed her shoulder as he might caress a fractious, frightened horse. "I'm here. I'll protect you. I have a lifetime of dealing with dark beings here or in any other dimension. We're here for a reason, that I know. And I don't feel that trying to find this green sphere is a bad thing. I feel Yellow Teeth nearby and that means he's going to be stalking me as usual, not you."

Leaning into his cupped hand on her shoulder, Shelly absorbed the strength and unexpected warmth from Colt. She closed her eyes briefly, whispering, "Thank you." She absorbed his continued touch. "You scare me, Colt, in some ways. In other ways, I feel like you're a knight from the Round Table here to protect me."

If he didn't remove his hand now, Colt wouldn't

be able to resist touching her graceful neck, threading his fingers through that mass of gleaming red-gold hair and then finding her mouth to kiss her. Never in his life had he been so mesmerized by a woman. In the past, he could remain immune to their charms, their guile, their bodies and the way they swayed when they walked. But not Shelly. Forcing his hand away, he managed a slight smile. "I'm no threat to you. I want to protect you, Shelly."

Searching his face, she realized that something magical had happened between them. Shelly didn't know why, but it had, and now Colt's rugged face was readable. She felt his sensitivity, his awareness, his raw need of her. And then, just as suddenly, Shelly watched him bring down a steel wall between them. All his warmth, his desire for her, vanished. In its place came an implacable look coupled with strength.

"You're not an easy man to understand."

"I'm complex," he agreed. But so was Shelly. Colt wanted to ask her a hundred questions. "But what about you? I don't feel you're an uncomplicated person, either."

Laughing, perhaps from the strain of the connection building between them, Shelly said, "Oh, compared to you, I'm quite simple."

Colt knew that wasn't true. Right now, he had to remain alert and stay focused on the mission. "We need to study the maps back in our hotel room and get an idea of what we're going to do tomorrow," he told her.

"I agree," Shelly murmured, somewhat reassured that Colt's defenses were not aimed at her, but rather his wanting to protect her. Shelly had never been trained in the art of psychic defense. Vortexes for the most part were simple, straightforward and not really dangerous at all—unlike spirits or men.

Colt stood up and motioned to the hotel. "Let's go to our rooms and rest for a while. I'd like to catch some quick shut-eye." He entertained the thought of one room, but said nothing. Understanding that Yellow Teeth hovered somewhere unseen yet watching, Colt wasn't about to leave himself open or Shelly defenseless, should the evil witch decide to take advantage of a romantic moment between them.

"Good idea," Shelly said, standing and smoothing out the fabric of her slacks.

Colt moved to her side. To hell with it. He slipped his hand beneath her elbow and guided her along the sidewalk. He wanted to touch her. He wanted her. All his training as a medicine man warned him not to engage her and yet he couldn't stop himself completely. Threading through the happy, chatting tourists walking along beside Lake Louise, Colt understood as never before that he was a shield for Shelly. Whatever was going to happen next, he had to be aware. There was no room for error.

Chapter 6

"Where are they going?" Victor growled. He stood up on a slight knoll above the canoe wharf the next morning. Fog slipped silently across the emerald lake at 6:00 a.m. Few tourists were up and about at this hour. He'd felt the *Taqe* awaken and watched as they had breakfast in the Wildflower Restaurant at the hotel. Then they'd donned their hiking gear and taken off long before the sun climbed above the peaks. At his side were Jeff and Lothar.

"They're bypassing the wharf," Lothar said.

Frowning, Victor rubbed his chin. They stepped

off the path and began to walk slowly along the edge of the lake. "They're looking for something."

Shrugging, Lothar said, "Let them do the dirty work. Then we'll swoop in and take the sphere at the right moment."

Victor nodded. "Exactly. We have cell phones as well as mental telepathy in order to stay in touch. Jeff, you do the tailing. Don't let them see you. Stay back. Note what they do. It won't take more than half a day to go around most of this lake."

"Yes, my lord," Jeff said. He had on a day pack, wore jeans, a green T-shirt and sturdy hiking boots.

"The only part of this lake that doesn't have a trail is down there," Lothar said, pointing beyond the wharf.

"And my guess is they are going to scour the shoreline on this side first," Victor said. "And if they don't find it there, they'll come back and pick up that canoe they rented yesterday."

"I'd give anything to see them find it," Jeff said.

Turning, Victor glared at him. "Don't lose your head, boy. If you think they've spotted it, you get a hold of us immediately. You don't take this into your own hands. Too much is at stake."

Riffling beneath the Dark Lord's censure, Jeff lowered his eyes. "I only meant, my lord, that the sphere probably isn't sitting on the shoreline of this lake. If it was, someone would have found it. I think they're looking for a sign as to where it might be located. Remember, the woman said she was would look for flowers along the shore?"

Victor decided Jeff wasn't as stupid as he'd assumed. "I believe she was lying, but I agree with you that they're looking for some kind of sign that might point them in the direction of the sphere. What, we don't know yet."

Jeff felt his anger cool as Victor treated him with more respect. "What about looking around specific rock formations? There's plenty of rock promontories around this lake."

Raising his brows, Victor gave Jeff a look of satisfaction. "Smart thinking, my boy. So, keep your binoculars handy and let's see what they stop and look at. Maybe we'll pick up a clue that way."

"Yes, my lord," Jeff murmured, feeling as though he was vindicated to a degree. The last thing he wanted was to be seen as stupid by the Dark Lord. He hadn't been in the *Tupay* realm that long and he had no wish to start off on the wrong foot with the boss.

"WAIT, COLT," Shelly cautioned. They had made a quarter of the circuit around Lake Louise. The sun climbed in the sky and the coolness of the morning disappeared like the fog that had hung across the lake earlier. She'd put out her hand and he stopped.

"You're feeling a vortex?" he asked.

"Do you feel it?" she asked, turning and giving him a smile. Colt looked focused, his eyes narrowed with intensity. She was beginning to realize he could never relax with the threat of the Skin Walker spirit. Her heart ached for him.

"Of course." Colt looked up and opened his senses more. "I'd say we're on the edge of it."

"I think we're right to assume that the emerald sphere could be near a vortex on a lakeshore. We just need to find those two boulders along with it."

"Right," Colt agreed, coming up to her shoulder. He peered over the lush grass bank. Below it were many pebbles and some rocks of varying sizes, shapes and colors. The lapping sound of the water soothed him. "I don't see two big boulders together. Do you?"

"No, darn it," Shelly said, frowning.

"Maybe there's more than one vortex on this lake?" he wondered. "Sometimes, because of the way the land formed," Colt said, gesturing around the lake, "there can be more than one."

"Local and regional vortexes can be anywhere," Shelly agreed, looking around the curve of the lake. As the sun moved higher in the sky, the water slowly turned from emerald to turquoise in color. The beauty all around her and having Colt so near was enough to make her yearn to throw her arms around his neck and kiss him. Last night had been a special hell for her. She'd done nothing but dream of kissing Colt and making love to him. As withdrawn and unapproachable as he was, she'd awakened at 3:00 a.m., gasping, with an ache in her lower body. She tried to tear her thoughts from the heat of her dream. "You see how those two mountains are situated above the lake?" she asked.

Colt looked to where she pointed. "Yes, I see them. That's a low point between them and often energy will run through such an area."

"They look like a saddle and are U-shaped." She turned and with her index finger pointed to the opposite side of the lake and the mountains in the distance. "And there's a low point between two mountains over there. In geomancy, low elevation areas between peaks are natural openings for earth energies to flow without obstruction. And that could give us more than one vortex here on this lake."

"Right on," Colt said. There was nothing to dislike about this woman who seemed to be such an idealist. The opposite of him. But then, Colt reminded himself, she came from a different world than he did. She had no training or defense knowledge of the dark side of the other worlds and dimensions. He did. Still, he allowed himself the pleasure of losing himself in her green, gold and brown eyes. They shone with an excitement and joy that infused him. In that moment, Colt realized Shelly was able to touch his heart as no other woman ever had.

"Well," she sighed, "it's possible that another local or regional line, called a Hartmann line, could be crossing this large corridor of energy. Where they cross, there's always a vortex."

"Reading the land is tough," Colt said, looking around. "We don't call these lines of energy by any name, but we feel them and know they are there."

"My father is a geomancer. He came by the skill naturally through our Irish bloodlines. All of his family 'walked the land' in Ireland. He taught me everything I know." Shelly smiled up at him. Colt wore his black hat. He had traded in his Western footwear for hiking boots. Reluctantly. There was something warm and simple about him that drew her like a magnet. She saw the heat banked in his blue eyes as he held her gaze. Oh, how badly she wanted to kiss that mouth of his! Shelly was glad he couldn't read her mind.

"I can see it would take years and a lot of travel to understand how ley lines worked with local Hartmann lines," he told her. "My father began teaching me about the energy patterns and lines when I was six years old."

"A dowser can easily locate them with dowsing rods," she told him. "And, yes, it's a lifelong learning."

Taking his hat off, Colt wiped his brow and settled the Stetson back on his head. He had a hard time keeping his eyes off Shelly. She was fetching in her jeans, a white long-sleeved blouse covered with a hot-pink nylon jacket. The color set off her red hair, tamed to a degree beneath her pink knit cap. Even July mornings were in the mid-forties in the middle of the Canadian Rockies. By noon, the temperature would bring a lovely seventy to eighty degrees and they could tuck their jackets and hats away in their day packs.

Pulling a bottle of water from her belt, Shelly drank deeply. Already she could see tourists coming out on the path around the lovely, long glacial lake. Fortunately they were far enough from the hotel that few people had wandered their way yet. Capping the bottle, she snugged it back into a net holder on her belt. "With this energy flowing through these mountains, I think the next vortex we might run into will be on that opposite shore." Shelly pointed to an area where there was no trail.

"We'll take that canoe when we're done hiking here and check it out," Colt said.

"Wouldn't it be lovely if the emerald sphere was over there?"

Colt grimaced. "Yes, it would. But if we find it, what do we do with it?"

"Well, I'm hoping you or I will have a dream that

tells us those things," Shelly said, skimming her thumbs beneath the straps of her pack.

"I like it here," Colt said, falling into step with her as she continued forward. "This is a great place to visit." If only the threat of Yellow Teeth weren't in the background. Colt felt himself wanting to open up, to allow his defenses to drop and simply enjoy time and space with Shelly. She infused him with joy, a rarity in his lifetime.

As they walked along the lakeshore, Colt shortened his stride for her. Sometimes, by accident, their hands would graze as they walked the narrowed trail. Each time, Colt absorbed that fleeting touch like the starving animal he was. Shelly reminded him of just how much he ached for a real relationship with a woman—to be able to open up, be vulnerable and share. But then anger rifled through him and he thought of Yellow Teeth. The Skin Walker had ruined his life in so many ways. Colt wished the cowardly witch would confront him once and for all. Only one of them would survive that confrontation. And Colt was tired of waiting. With a woman like Shelly around him, he wanted—needed—to have a real life, a love, a dream of a future with a woman who made him happy and vice versa.

Colt felt the telltale rippling sensation that told him a small vortex was nearby. As he drew closer to the center of it, about fifty feet up the bank, he stopped. "This is a male vortex," he told Shelly. "Let's look carefully around the bank here."

He got down on his hands and knees to look below the overhang. Searching the shoreline, Colt saw only small, colorful pebbles. They had been ground smooth and were slightly rounded or made oval by the sheer weight and force of the Ice Age glaciers. "Nope," he grunted, sitting back on his heels, "they're not here."

"Bummer," Shelly muttered, holding out her hand to Colt. "I feel like we've just begun a long search." Her fingers curled around his and he stood up. He didn't want to release her fingers but he knew he had to. Any reason to touch Shelly was a good one. He asked himself where this was going. His life had been indelibly stamped out for him. As he watched Shelly remove her knit cap and her red hair fell softly against her shoulders, his heart ached. What would it be like to tame that red hair of hers? Shelly quickly ran her fingers through the strands and smoothed them into place.

"Vortex number two," he said, standing at her side. His arm yearned to curve around her shoulders. Colt trembled inwardly. He was so close, so close to doing it.

"Maybe a number three," Shelly said, taking off her pack and placing the knit cap and jacket inside it. "I love the beauty here. But I live in absolute fear of that sorcerer who wants the emerald."

"I don't blame you," Colt said, turning around. He felt as if they were being watched. Scanning the shore and the slight knolls that proliferated with thick stands of fir, Colt couldn't spot anyone.

"Are you sensing Yellow Teeth? Is he near?" Her voice went a little high with tension.

"Yes. We're being followed and watched. It is Yellow Teeth."

Shivering, Shelly said, "I've been too focused on finding the vortex energy. I'm glad you're aware of him."

Colt's stomach clenched with anger against his old nemesis. He tried to sound confident for Shelly's sake because he didn't want her to feel afraid. "We're not going to be blindsided. Keep concentrating on finding the vortexes with me. We'll be all right."

Reaching out, Shelly touched his arm. "You're a big, bad guard dog, Colt."

Her touch electrified him, and his body went hard between his thighs. Groaning inwardly, Colt wondered if Shelly realized her touch sent fire coursing through him. Her lips were parted, begging to be kissed. By him.

All he could do was agree with her and tear his gaze away. "*Your* guard dog."

As she felt heat flow from her neck into her cheeks, Shelly released her hand from his upper arm. The look in Colt's eyes at her touch stunned her. His blue eyes narrowed instantly. She felt a naked desire from him embracing her. It was a wonderful feeling, filled with promise. Its raw primal quality sent Shelly into connection with her own womanly core. What would it be like to make love to Colt? She knew it would be special. Wild. Natural, like him.

Chastising herself, Shelly realized this morning just how powerfully she was taken with Colt. Oh, it was nothing he did or said; it was just him. Okay, maybe that wasn't the truth. The way he looked at her made her yearn for him in every possible way. Colt was like decadent chocolate walking unexpectedly into her life. Any candy, especially eye candy like him, had to be savored fully, but that was all, she sternly told herself.

"Come on," she said, gesturing for him to follow. "We have more ground to cover before lunch."

JEFF STOOD WELL-HIDDEN in the grove of small and large firs. When the male *Taqe* turned and looked directly at him, it had scared the hell out of him. Frozen like a deer, Jeff heaved a sigh of relief when Black turned away and paid attention to his partner. Had they found what they were looking for? He waited impatiently until they were out of sight.

Jeff bounded down to the bank where the woman had gotten on her hands and knees, but Jeff could see nothing of interest. Sitting back on the heels of his hiking boots, he was aware of turbulent energy around him. What was it? Then he realized it was a tornado-like energy spinning near where he knelt— a vortex. Frowning, Jeff wondered about that. Back in his room he had the woman's book, *How to Find a Vortex.* It had been on the *New York Times* bestseller list for months. He vowed to read it tonight since it could give him more insight into what the team was doing.

"THERE!" SHELLY SHOUTED from the bow of the red canoe. She lifted her paddle out of the smooth, quiet water of Lake Louise. They were ten feet offshore and slowly paralleling the bank where no trail existed. "Can you feel it? A vortex! A few feet ahead."

Colt sat in the stern of the canoe. He dug deeply into the water with his paddle and guided it closer to shore. "It's another male vortex." Shelly had been dead accurate about the possibility of it being here. At least in this area, they were true teammates with the same amount of experience and knowledge.

"A little stronger than the first one we ran into." She craned her neck and narrowed her eyes. The early-afternoon sunlight was in her eyes. She took a baseball cap and fitted it low over her eyes in order to see better.

Colt saw nothing along the shore that resembled the two boulders they were seeking. The strength of this vortex was noticeably different.

Colt twisted around and looked at the geography of the area surrounding the lake. "Placement of a local or regional vortex has everything to do with determining its strength," he remarked. The canoe's bow scraped the pebbled bottom near the shore.

Shelly anxiously looked along the bank. No boulders. Just pretty, smooth and rounded pebbles instead. "I think because the main energy line runs between those two mountains it makes this vortex more powerful."

The paddle resting across his thighs, Colt grinned. "Yes," he agreed. It was a secret pleasure to watch her move. Like those of a graceful deer, her motions flowed from one act to the next. What would it be like to have her hands flow over his naked body like that? The thought made him burn.

Turning around, Shelly sat back on the wooden seat. "We've only got about half a mile to go. I don't see where there could be another vortex based upon the shapes of the land. Do you?"

"No, but we'll scour every inch, anyway," Colt promised. "Can you push us off with the paddle?"

Nodding, Shelly carefully used the paddle to ease

the canoe off the pebbly shoal until they were once more out into deeper water. "My guess is that whatever lake we saw in our dreams, it wasn't this one."

"I saw a long, oval lake," Colt said. "Looking at the topo map, there's plenty of them in this area besides Lake Louise."

"I know," Shelly murmured, stressed over the fact there were so many. "I wish our dreams had been more specific."

Looking up, Colt saw a red-tailed hawk and its mate flying in ever higher spirals above the lake. Their rust-red tails were beautiful against the deep blue of the summer sky. "Mine was general, too," Colt said, paddling and enjoying the bobbing motion of the canoe.

"This seems so impossible," Shelly said, glum.

"Cheer up. Once we get done here, we'll go back to the Wildflower Restaurant for some iced tea. We'll look at the topo map and decide what lake we should look at next."

That perked her up. Whether she wanted to admit it or not, Shelly longed for downtime to get to know Colt better. Laughing, she said over her shoulder, "I can hardly wait!"

Neither could Colt. Any excuse to be near Shelly, to hear her breathy voice, to catch her fleeting scent that reminded him of sweet honey, was worth it.

MIDAFTERNOON IN THE Wildflower Restaurant was quiet compared to the breakfast rush, Shelly thought. She sat at Colt's elbow, sipping iced tea with lemon. They spread out the topographic map and she inched closer, inhaling Colt's scent. He'd rolled up the long sleeves of the dark green cowboy shirt to just below his elbows. His hands were work-worn, and Shelly yearned to have those fingers slide across her skin with reverence. Colt seemed so aloof and guarded. She could feel his attraction but he didn't seem willing to give in to it. Shelly struggled to shelve her desire for him. How could she fall for another man? It was too easy to forget her rules when Colt's confidence and masculine strength were so alluring. He reminded her of these tall, rugged Rocky Mountains in so many ways. Colt was unlike any other man she'd ever been drawn to. Maybe that was a good sign.

"So? What do you think?" she asked him, tapping the topo map with her index finger. "The next closest oblong lake is Lake Agnes. It's northwest of Lake Louise."

Colt followed her slim index finger on the map. "It says there's a teahouse at the lake." He recalled his dream and told her about the log restaurant he'd seen.

Shelly craned over the map. "So there is! It looks as though we could hike the very long and steep trail up to Lake Agnes. Once we get there, it is an easy walk around half of it. The other half has no trail and it will be rough going."

"Then we could stop at that teahouse and rest," Colt said. "It means I can trust my dream. I couldn't imagine a teahouse in these mountains."

"Actually," Shelly said with a grin, tapping the map again, "there's another one indicated on the Plain of Six Glaciers Trail that's southwest of Lake Agnes."

"We don't have to hike out to it," Colt said, looking over at her. Colt had the wild, unbidden urge to tame an errant lock of her red hair. He was so taken with her, but he had to keep reminding himself that it couldn't be. Not ever. Sadness riffled through him as he neatly folded up the map. Sometimes Colt didn't like his life. Right now, he was rankled by it. Shelly was a constant reminder to him of what he couldn't have. But dammit, he desperately wanted it now. Right now.

Colt stole a look over at Shelly as she sipped her iced tea. She was so pretty, alive and magical. Never mind she was an expert on vortexes. He was simply enjoying spending time in her company. When had he *ever* had this kind of pleasure? *Never.* Colt tucked the map away in his day pack. For whatever reason, amidst the danger and threat of dying, Colt had found a woman he dared to dream of. Dared to want a future with. But how? Yellow Teeth might try to possess Shelly and kill her just as he had killed his sister, Mary.

Chapter 7

"Did you find anything?" Victor asked as he sat with Lothar and Jeff in the lounge. Most people were at one of the many fine restaurants at the hotel and they were alone in the sumptuous area. They huddled together, looking like a football team on a field of battle.

"My lord," Jeff said, "I went to every spot they stopped at and surveyed."

Lothar nodded. "Jeff took me to them and the only thing they had in common was a vortex at each site."

Rubbing his chin, Victor muttered, "There must be a tie to vortexes. That's obvious. The sphere did not show me a vortex. Only those two boulders."

"What about the flowers?" Jeff inquired. He instantly regretted his question as Victor snapped up his head and glared at him.

"Fool! That was a lie on their part. A ruse. You have to get used to *Taqe* lying to cover their tracks."

"I didn't think *Taqe* lied," Jeff said.

Snorting, Victor said, "Oh, they lie! They will do anything to get these emerald spheres. They're no white knights, either, as much as they'd like to think they are."

From where they sat, Jeff could smell bread baking at the Wildflower Restaurant. He inhaled and savored the fragrance. Being in body was such a treat. He looked forward to every meal as never before. "How many vortexes are there around these lakes in this vicinity?" he wondered.

Lothar grunted. He sat up and rubbed his hands down the length of his jeans. "That is a real question, isn't it?"

"That is our dilemma," Victor growled unhappily. "There are many vortexes in this area. Since we're clairvoyant, they're easy for us to spot."

"The question then becomes—are they looking for a particular vortex along a particular lakeshore along with those boulders?" Jeff said, relieved that Victor's withering glare disappeared. This time, he'd posed the correct question.

"Exactly."

"I saw them earlier at the restaurant with the topo map open," Lothar said. "I couldn't get close enough to see what they were examining on their map. And we can't probe their minds or they'll know we're here and that will blow our cover."

"Doesn't matter," Victor grumbled. "All we have to do is follow and watch. It's obvious to me that they don't know on which lakeshore this emerald sphere exists, either. They're searching and looking just like we are."

"At least that gives us a chance to get it," Lothar said. "If they don't know where it is, all we have to do is keep tailing them."

"On another topic," Victor said, "did you notice their auras are changing? The pink colors in their astral fields have increased?" He rubbed his hands together and chuckled. "They're sexually attracted to one another. And that will cause them to lose focus." He hooked a thumb in the direction of the restaurant. "It's happening again as it did with the other *Taqe* who were at the Great Serpent Mound. Lovebirds. Perfect for us because they're going to leave us an opening to drive a truck through at the right moment."

"I've noticed a deepening red color in the male *Taqe*'s aura," Lothar said.

"Even better," Victor snickered. "Men tend to think between their legs, unlike women. He will be our weak spot. Just as Robert Cramer was the weak member in the last team, Colt Black is going to give us a similar opening." And then his smile widened. "Besides, Yellow Teeth wants a shot at him first. He has to remain far away or the *Taqe* male will sense his presence. At the right time, I'm going to take Yellow Teeth off his coyote leash and he can kill him."

ON THE WAY BACK to their rooms, Colt felt his heart was so open that he was helpless to control it any longer. Shelly was sunshine to his world of threats. As they walked, their hands occasionally touching, Colt agonized. He'd been a perfect gentleman throughout dinner, even though all he could do was focus on her lips. When they curved in a smile, his heart soared like a hawk flying toward the sun. She possessed such beauty, the kind that didn't need enhancement. Colt found himself admiring her confidence. There was a guileless nature to her that drew him.

Slowing to a halt, Colt couldn't stop himself. He reached out and pulled Shelly around to face him. When she lifted her lashes to gaze wonderingly up at him, he went weak inside. "I don't know what's happening," he told her in a husky voice. "All I want to do is kiss you."

Touched by his sudden vulnerability, Shelly hesitated, then lifted her hand and slid it across his cheek. Mistake or not, she followed her pounding heart. "Kiss me, Colt," She settled her hands on his chest and leaned upward.

Colt felt her lips settle against his own. Shelly's mouth was soft and pliant. Groaning internally, Colt swept his arms around her and brought her fully against him. He captured her and tasted her. Just the grazing touch of her soft skin against his sent a keening ache through him. Her fragrance was a combination of fir, fresh mountain air and a sweetness that was only Shelly. Fire ignited within Colt as he deepened their kiss. Feeling her hands creep upward and slide around his neck told him so much.

Breath growing ragged, Colt felt her need matching his with a ferocity that shook him to his soul. And when she moaned, the sound sweetly reverberated through him, and every cell in his body responded. Framing her face with his hands, Colt absorbed her soft lips, her scent, the tickling sensation as the red strands of her hair grazed his cheek and temple.

The pressure of her breasts, the way her arms encircled his neck, all conspired against Colt. He wanted Shelly in every way. And yet, at the moment of greatest realization came the terrible, sinking sensation. Tearing his mouth from hers, Colt stared down into her half-closed eyes. Colt saw love in them—for him. How was it possible to fall in love this quickly? He gripped her shoulders and gently eased her away from his hard, throbbing body.

"Shelly…" His voice broke. Colt stared darkly down at her.

"Oh, Colt," she whispered, her voice filled with regret. "I've tried to be immune to you." She gave him a confused look.

"We shouldn't have kissed. I can't do this, Shelly. I want to, but I know I can't."

Whispering his name, Shelly stepped out of his grip and leaned against the wall next to the door. "It's the Skin Walker threat, isn't it?" Shelly could feel him being torn apart by his own personal need and the dangerous life he led. Reaching out, she touched his jaw. "From the moment I saw you, I was drawn to you." She pressed her fingers over her heart. "I see your struggle with the Skin Walker stalking you and it hurts me."

Resting his hands on his hips, Colt stared hard at her. "I'm torn, Shelly." He wanted to say, *I want you so badly I can taste it*. He stayed silent and held her warm hazel gaze. Clearly, she was just as shocked over the kiss as he was. "My relationships have been short. I've deliberately walked away from the women I was attracted to."

"Why would you give up happiness?" Shelly asked, searching his dark blue eyes. "Is it all because of the threat of the Skin Walker?" Shelly could understand that up to a point. She'd never tasted or faced evil as Colt had. Further, he was so tight-lipped about it, she had little to go on.

Colt fought to not raise his arms once more and pull Shelly into his embrace. "I haven't told you ev-erything." He felt as if his heart had turned into a nest of angry snakes. The emotional pain of telling Shelly the truth wrestled with his tribe's mantra never to speak of evil. To do so brought it to the person who spoke of it.

"Then tell me," she countered, hoping to coax out the storm she saw in his eyes. "I know I'm not trained to look for evil like you are. I'm not afraid to listen to you, Colt." Her voice became more firm and knowing. "I'm not into short-term anything. I've been burned by every man I fell for. I don't have a great track record of choosing the right guys, either. I can't keep making the same mistake. Help me understand."

Colt took a step away and looked up and down the quiet hall. In many ways, he had to tell her. They were on a mission together and needed a foundation of trust. So without hesitating, he told his story, his fear and the loss of Mary. Shelly's face had gone white by the time he'd finished the terrible tragic tale. Her copper freckles stood out across her nose and cheeks. Her eyes were wide and filled with a mixture of shock and sympathy. "So, now you know everything, Shelly. I'm a dangerous man to be around for any length of time. Yellow Teeth relentlessly stalks me." He held her gaze, hoping she understood the danger. "I'm afraid that he'll attack you, not me. I know how to defend myself against a possession attack. You don't. And Mary wasn't trained to do that, either, but I was. That's why Yellow Teeth went after her first. She was a lamb going to slaughter."

Gulping, Shelly stood, hands clenched in one another in front of her. "And that's why you don't stay with a woman very long."

Nodding his head, Colt said, "Yes. I'm putting no one at risk of this Skin Walker killing again."

"What a horrible threat you have to live with."

"If Yellow Teeth even thinks I'm attracted to you or want you…he may set his sights on you and not me." It took everything he had to stop staring at her mouth. How badly Colt wanted to kiss Shelly again. *Impossible.*

"Well," she said, "if we're able to find the emerald, do you think it can help us with the threat of Yellow Teeth?"

"I don't know," Colt muttered. Placing his hands on his hips, he inhaled deeply and released the breath. "Shelly, by being around me, you're in life-and-death danger. It's that simple. And you have no training to defend yourself against evil. That's why I've tried to hold you at arm's length since we met."

"I didn't know whether you even liked me."

"Of course I like you. But the moment I allow my shield to dissolve, he'd be here in a heartbeat, plunging in through the top of my head and taking over my body. He'd cut the silver cord to my spirit and force me out of the physical realm."

Shivering, Shelly leaned against the wall and wrapped her arms against her chest. "That sounds awful." Shelly wanted to hug him fiercely, but she didn't dare. "Can you teach me how to defend myself against an attack like that?"

"I can show you some things, but not enough to keep you safe a hundred percent of the time," he admitted in a reflective tone.

She swallowed hard and held his narrowed blue gaze. "I don't want anything to happen to either of us while we're hunting for that sphere. I'm a fast learner, Colt. I'm not afraid."

Colt nodded, seeing the determination in the set of her lips, the frown between her brows. "I'll teach you what I can." He had never dreamed of meeting someone like Shelly. "I'll keep us safe," he promised her.

Hope moved through Shelly. "Just give me a chance to learn. I don't want to be a weak link to you."

Her frustration came through loud and clear. One corner of his mouth hitched upward. Thrusting his hands into the pockets of his jeans, Colt murmured, "One thing you haven't been to me is a ball and chain, Shelly."

"I hope not. I have other strong paranormal skills in place to help you."

"Yes, you do," Colt acknowledged. "You aren't a beginner, but fighting evil means having an internal strength of spirit, too. And you don't have that, Shelly. You can get it, build it over time, but you won't be able to have enough in place right now, no matter what I show you."

"It will have to be enough," Shelly said, trying to curb her impatience. A long time ago Shelly had realized she had a type A personality—she raced at top speed all the time. Colt was a type B—laid-back and not caught up in her hurry, hurry world. She wanted to know everything immediately. More than that, she wanted to kiss him again. Getting romantically involved wasn't the brightest thing to do. If she kissed him, it would only create more pressure on herself and that was not what Shelly needed.

"Besides," she added, "we have to find this emerald. We can't get sidetracked knowing Yellow Teeth is around just waiting to attack."

"I can feel him around, Shelly. I haven't seen

him, but he's stalking us. Usually, he's close, but for whatever reason, he seems to be far away right now." His brows dipped. "And I don't understand why he's hanging back. He's never done that before."

Tilting her head, Shelly asked, "What do you mean?"

"The Skin Walker has always been close and I could see him. Now, he's out of my clairvoyant sight. It could be a new tactic he's trying on me," Colt said, looking up and down the quiet hall once again. He wanted no one to hear their conversation.

"I'll shoulder just as much of the load as I can." Shelly tried to show confidence.

He smiled tentatively. "A wild horse always surges ahead," he told her.

Shelly gazed at him for a long moment. "Is that how you see me? I'm a wild horse?"

"Your red hair reminds me of the mane of a war-bonnet paint mare that runs in our area with a wild herd of mustangs. When she's running, her mane is the same color as your hair."

"She must be very beautiful."

You are beautiful. Colt caught the words that begged to be spoken to her. "She is. I enjoy watching the herd running along the mesa outside our small community. It makes my heart sing."

How badly Shelly wanted to taste Colt's un-shielded vulnerable side for just a few minutes longer. "Maybe she's in your life to remind you that you can have the same freedom she does."

The words, spoken so quietly, like a breeze through the halls of his mind, startled him. Colt eyed her sharply, then sighed. This woman had a tremendous amount of insight because of her clairvoyant abilities. "Until I can confront Yellow Teeth," he said, "I am in a prison of sorts. I've been waiting for years for him to attack me."

"Can't you stalk *him?*"

"No. I wish I could, but I don't have that kind of ability. I have to wait for him to charge."

Again, a chill worked its way up through Shelly. "You *will* win, won't you?" Suddenly, Shelly couldn't conceive of life without Colt in it. He was powerful. A warrior. And she believed that good overcame bad. But did it really? Was that her idealism speaking?

"I don't know. No one knows until the battle begins. I know I'm strong in spirit. But so is he. We're evenly matched." And then, more grimly, the expression in his eyes distant, "but I have one thing on my side he doesn't. I have a murderous rage toward him. This will make me stronger."

Shelly felt the cold resolve within him, along with his armor. The man who had talked with her in this hall was gone. At least now she understood why. Her lips tingled wildly in memory of that mouth upon hers.

"Listen, we need sleep," Shelly said. In her heart of hearts, she wanted to say, *Come to bed with me, Colt. Be at my side. Let me love you. Let me show you the freedom that you can have...* All dreams, Shelly realized, a ribbon of sadness moving through her heart. If Colt dropped those walls, he was vulnerable to Yellow Teeth. And the shape-shifter could attack him at that moment. Shelly wrestled with her own feelings.

Pulling his hands out of his pockets, Colt said, "You're right." Without thinking, he reached out and slid his hand behind her head, his fingers tangling within the soft strands of her red hair. Leaning down, he pressed a chaste kiss to her brow. "Tonight, I will dream of you, my wild mustang woman...." It would be all he would ever have: dreams of Shelly. If Yellow Teeth even suspected he was falling in love with Shelly, the Skin Walker would go after her first. And he couldn't stand the idea of a second person in his life being ripped away from him. Not ever.

Chapter 8

By 6:00 a.m. the next morning, Shelly and Colt were on the trail leading to Lake Agnes. The dawn was crisp with fog blanketing Lake Louise. They moved steadily upward as they left it behind and hiked toward a much smaller area nestled deep in the Rockies. At this time, only the brave were out hiking or jogging on this particularly steep trail. Shelly cherished the quiet moments. The jays squawked and followed them from tree to tree as they went into the forest.

The path was wide enough for Colt to walk at her side. She gave him a quick smile. Just being with him sent warmth cascading through her. She felt his protectiveness.

"How did your dad take to you being a vortex hunter?" Colt wondered. "Did he have a dream for you to do something else? Maybe became an investment banker like him?"

"My dad already had me taking over his investment banking business when he retired." She laughed and saw his somber and serious expression lighten a little. "My mother wanted me to be a teacher like herself."

"So, you had your parents each wanting you to walk their path in a certain career."

"Yes, just like your father groomed you to become a medicine man."

Colt nodded and watched the shafts of sunlight cascading on the mountain before them. The granite was blue and only a bit of snow was at the summits. The sky was a light blue at this time of morning. "Did you wrestle with this?"

"Their expectations tore me apart when I was young, Colt. Of course I wanted to please them. They would tell me the positives of being an investment banker and a teacher. They focused on a good living, the ability to buy a house and be economically secure. What about your father? What did he tell you when he wanted you to become a medicine man?"

The path was smooth with evergreens on either side. Colt watched where he put his feet. He felt Yellow Teeth, but he was still at a distance and this confounded Colt. The Skin Walker was just waiting for him to drop his protection completely. "Since the first day I can remember, my father told me I was going to become a medicine man. I don't remember anything different."

"Told you? Or asked if you wanted to be one?"

He gave her a strange look. "Did your parents ask you if you wanted to be an investment banker or teacher? Or did they tell you that you had to choose between one of those careers?"

Shelly smiled a bit. Her breath was coming a little faster as they made the slow ascent through the dark, cool woodlands. "They didn't tell me, Colt. They always talked about how it would be great if I'd be a banker or a teacher. They never told me I had to be one or the other."

"I see."

"But they still pressured me. And it was uncomfortable. I'm sure it was for you, too. Or did you always want to be a medicine man?"

Colt shrugged. "It's different in the Navajo culture. A medicine man is considered equal to the chief or leader of the tribe. It is a very responsible position, and one that is respected by others."

"I see," Shelly said. They broke out of the woods.

In front of them was a steep, winding set of stairs. Above it stood the stone and log teahouse. As they climbed to the top, out of breath, they saw a small oval lake surrounded by the gray and blue granite mountains. There were swathes of snow here and there. The rib-like horizontal striations on the summits had given this area the name *beehives*. Agnes sat at the bottom of the talus slopes like a blue jewel. A few clumps of evergreens could be seen at some points of the lakeshore.

Pointing toward the small oval lake, she said, "You remember the saying, 'as above, so below'? Look at the reflection of the mountain across the glassy water's surface. If you didn't know where you were, you might not know which was real and which wasn't."

Colt appreciated the incredible beauty of the reflection. "Yes, my father taught me that. Seeing it like this gives it new meaning. Where are we, really? Is that reflection more real than where we are presently standing? Do we really know?"

"That's what it's like between the different dimensions. Things are the same. When I'm seeing in the fourth dimension with my third eye—" and she touched the center of her brow "—I've learned to reorient myself so I know what is in that dimension and where I'm standing physically in this dimension."

"Yes, I agree. Still, to see this law of our universe to be repeated here in the third dimension is to remind us that there are other worlds just like ours."

"I'm sure Yellow Teeth feels the same way about us."

Colt grunted. "Yes. He's more dangerous to us in spirit because he can move at will in the blink of a thought between the dimensions. Us? We'll have to trudge one step at a time toward our goal because we are in body."

"We can't just think it and be there?" She chuckled, enjoying him. Looking into Colt's blue eyes, she found happiness lurking in their shadowy depths. Intuitively, she knew he liked being with her. Last night, Shelly had lain awake for a long time thinking about their conversation outside her hotel room. And about their wonderful, melting kiss. It had taken hours before her body settled down and stopped wanting him. There was nothing to dislike about Colt. He was sensitive and philosophical behind that wall. Shelly liked those traits and they matched her own. None of the men she'd chosen before had had a similar background to her. Maybe that was her mistake and why they had all ended up in heartbreak. Yet, a huge armored wall stood between them with Yellow Teeth at the center of it all.

Now, as Shelly drowned in the blueness of his

eyes, she felt a new stirring in her heart. One that she'd never felt before. Was this real love? The kind her parents had talked about? She'd fallen in love before. Or thought she had—with the wrong kind of man. What she was feeling now for Colt was so different, beautiful and haunting.

Confused, Shelly gently broke contact with his gaze and turned toward the lake far below them. Lake Agnes was actually a large oval lake although it appeared pear-shaped because the eastern end was smaller.

She had to have time to absorb these new tendrils that were alive and clamoring in her fast-beating heart. It wasn't the altitude that was making her pulse race. It was that tender look Colt had just shared with her for a split second before he grew distant once more. It made her breathless to see the real Colt.

Colt sensed Shelly's need of him. It was an incredible feeling much like a gentle breeze riffling upward from his toes to the top of his head. He discovered at precious, unexpected moments like this he could see the gold dancing in the depths of her green-and-brown eyes. And that gold was her desire for him. When he'd shifted his gaze to her parted lips, she'd turned away and looked down at the lake. Yes, they both remembered their hot, fusing kiss from last night. He wanted more, much more. For now, Colt gently put aside need and focused on the lake below.

"We need to start exploring," he said. The bank on one side had a well-worn trail and they could walk along the bank with ease. The other side had no trail and was rocky. He pointed toward a spiral of smoke coming from within the trees at the northern end of the lake. "That's the teahouse I saw in my dream."

Shelly brightened. "Great! I could use a cup of hot tea or coffee. We've earned that after this climb."

Without thinking, Colt reached out and touched her blazing red cheek. Hiking always made Shelly's cheeks flush, which did nothing but emphasize the beauty of her large, intelligent eyes. "Come on, my wild mustang woman, let's go." He grazed her cheek with his fingers. Oh, how he wanted to kiss her. His patience was thinning.

He dropped his hand and moved to one side of the path. Fortunately, it was well-maintained by the forest service who removed rocks to prevent people from accidentally walking on them and rolling into a fall. Since there was enough room for two people, he gestured for her to walk beside him. They agreed to search the small lake first and then reward themselves with coffee at the teahouse.

Shelly felt the tingly sensation upon her cheek. Colt's touch was completely unexpected. Until this moment, Shelly hadn't realized how much she wanted him to touch her again. And, for a split second, she almost leaned up on her toes to place a quick kiss on his mouth. But to what purpose? As long as Colt fought the Skin Walker, there would be no room for her in his life.

The knowledge was bittersweet as they ambled down the curving path across the slippery talus slope. Shelly wanted to return to the thread of their topic back in the forest. "Are you curious how I became a vortex hunter instead of an investment banker or teacher?"

"Yes, I am," he said. "I wonder how anyone could break away from their parents' demands to follow their dream."

"I wasn't breaking away from what my parents wanted for me. I had this calling," she said, touching her heart. "Throughout our family's history, we have had the Sight. When my parents brought me into the park for picnics and weekends, I was always searching out places of good-feeling energy. Over the years when they saw my passion for finding energy, which were vortexes or Hartmann lines, they realized I had a unique paranormal skill."

"A calling?"

"Yes," she said, giving him a quick smile. "It's my passion, too. Whenever my family drove from

Canmore into Banff National Park, I became so excited."

"So, as a little girl you were like a butterfly? Only you weren't landing on flowers, but seeking and finding these interesting energies upon the land instead?"

"Exactly," Shelly said with a laugh. "Everyone has a passion, Colt. All my parents had to say was *Banff* and I turned into their wild child."

"Or maybe your passion triggered your wild-mustang sense of freedom?" he guessed.

"When you follow your passion, freedom automatically comes with it," Shelly agreed.

"How did your parents figure out what you were doing every time you came out here to the park?"

"My parents knew about vortexes. My grandmother back in Ireland was what they called a 'walker of the land.' She'd made quite a name for herself in Ireland. People hired her to walk their land. Sometimes they wanted to build a home on a specific site of land, and they'd ask her to come to find out if the lines of energy that crisscrossed it were good or bad. No one wanted to build a home where there was a negative line of energy. It's very unhealthy. People would get very sick and some would die."

"That's interesting," Colt murmured. "I've run into negative energy areas on our res, too."

Halting at a slight promontory that overlooked Agnes, Shelly was glad for the rest. The high altitude made her heart pound even on the descent toward the lake. "I'm sure walking the land has many labels," Shelly said. "Are your medicine people aware of this technique?"

Colt shook his head. "Some are. Mostly, our tradition is in creating sand paintings and singing songs so that patients may get well."

"That is the wonder of our world, Colt. So many beautiful ways to help people and heal the land. My grandmother knew where ancient battles had been fought on the land, what lines of energy, if any, ran through an area, or if a discarnate spirit was wandering around."

Frowning, Colt muttered, "Spirits…"

"In your world, they are to be feared," Shelly said. "In my world, they are merely lost souls who haven't moved on to the light after dying. They remain in a place for a reason. My grandmother would tell their spouses were still alive and they remained here on Earth to care for them from the Other Side. Sometimes, the spirit was attached to a possession such as a house, an orchard or whatever they valued and didn't want to leave it after dying."

"And your grandmother was able to convince these spirits to leave?"

"Oh, yes," Shelly said. "She was a wonderful

persuader of sorts. She painted such a beautiful, loving picture of the world of light that they wanted to leave. The person's land or home became calm and quiet once more and the spirit was also in a good place. It was a win-win for everyone."

With a shake of his head, Colt said, "You and your family are very brave people. When Navajo see spirits, we run to our hogan, bar the door and stay inside. Spirits can't get inside our hogans but they can walk around the outsides and peek through the windows. I remember when I was about four years old and I was visiting my uncle's hogan near Chinle. I was just falling asleep and suddenly I saw the face of a ghost of an old Navajo who had just died pressed up against the window next to where I was lying. It frightened me so much I screamed. My father came and held me. I told him what I'd seen. That was when he told me that ghosts could not enter our homes. After sunset, ghosts come out. That is why when the sun goes down, we remain indoors."

"Wow," Shelly said, "that must have scared the daylights out of you. It would me, too."

"My focus is on Yellow Teeth, who I know is stalking us. The spirits of the dead are different and far less of a threat than a Skin Walker. If we discover this emerald, my gut tells me Yellow Teeth will confront me."

Reaching out, Shelly touched his upper arm. "Colt, I have a story to tell you. I was taught by my grams that when a malevolent spirit tries to attack you, you send it loving energy. It's the only human emotion it can't overcome. The old axiom 'love conquers all' has some teeth to it." She smiled and added, "Pardon the pun."

Colt saw she was sincere. "I don't know how you could love a sorcerer." There was no way he could send the Skin Walker love. Shelly's expression was filled with concern. "I just can't imagine trying to get to my love when I'm in a state of rage and wanting to destroy Yellow Teeth's spirit. How can anyone?"

"None of us do until we're challenged by it," Shelly told him, dropping her hand. If she didn't, she would walk into the circle of Colt's arms and kiss him once again. "I worry about it, too. Can I send Yellow Teeth love if I'm attacked by him? I don't know. But I do know I'm going to try should it happen. Love is the most powerful emotion in all the worlds. It is the only force that can save our lives if we are confronted."

Unhappily, Colt nodded. "It's not going to work with a Skin Walker."

"Nothing in this life is easy. I think you know that."

Grudgingly, Colt nodded. "I do." He was beginning to hate Yellow Teeth in a way he never had. Now, as never before, Colt felt the imprisonment he'd lived within. What he wanted was Shelly. He wanted to be himself around her, not the man behind the protective energy armor.

Turning, Shelly gazed across at Lake Agnes. They had walked halfway down the one side of the lake. The sun skimmed the tops of the Rockies, and the temperature was finally changing. She was just getting warm and didn't want to take off her coat yet. "One thing we have to remember, Colt. We have one another. How we feel for one another is a protection in itself." She wanted to say, *We are falling in love,* but didn't dare mouth those words.

Colt wouldn't dispute her softly spoken words. Without knowing why, he felt powerfully for Shelly. Not that he'd ever been in love to say, "This is love," but the feelings deep in his heart told him it might be. "Maybe because we care for one another, that is a possible antidote to a sorcerer?" he teased.

"Of course it is," she said with conviction. "I like being your friend, Colt." Every cell of her being knew she was lying. So long as the shadow of the deadly Skin Walker hovered over them, Shelly knew she couldn't tell Colt the truth—she was falling in love with him.

"I do, too."

Hearing the unhappiness in his tone, Shelly whispered, "Colt, just let things be. Our minds can mess with us. We have to have faith in an unknown future." She tapped the left side of her head. "Have you read Dr. Jill Bolte-Taylor's book *A Stroke of Insight?*"

"One of my aunts is reading the book."

"Borrow her copy when you get home," Shelly told him. "This amazing woman is a brain neuro-anatomist who suffered a major stroke at age thirty-seven on the left side of her brain." Shelly tapped her head. "And it took her eight years to recover, but she did. And now, in her book she destroys many of the myths about stroke survivors. Equally important, she has made stunning and amazing new awareness about the right and left hemispheres of our brains. The left side tries to anchor us only to this world. Our right side tries to open us up to the love and connection we have with all things seen and unseen in all the dimensions."

"So, I'm letting my left brain hold me in fear of Yellow Teeth?" Colt knew it was so much more than that. The threat was real.

"Yes, you are. Your right brain already knows that love is here and now." She indicated the path. "Colt, you can recognize the patterns containing threats of dying and stop playing them. Eventually, the left brain understands it can't play that old tape anymore and quiets down."

"That's an amazing way to look at life," he conceded. "I think I'd like to stay in my right brain. The Navajo believe all things are connected and related."

"Yes, and I bet you're right-brain dominant because you show such a reverence and connection with all of life. I see it in your aura and I feel it around you. It's just that some things fed into your left brain, whose job it is to tie you solidly to this time and space. They run a loop of memories that aren't really healthy for you and keep you imprisoned."

Colt shook his head. "I don't want to argue with you, Shelly. Yellow Teeth is not a figment of my imagination. Your idealism isn't countered by reality as my life has been." He saw her deflate beneath his words. So he gentled his tone. "I wish I had your idealism, Shelly. I really do. But that's not how it happened."

"That's the beauty of relationships," Shelly said. "Everyone is different. We have to look at where we agree." Seeing the pensive look on his features, Shelly felt the tug-of-war going on inside Colt. "We each have our own reality, Colt. And sometimes, one person's experiences or beliefs can touch your own. And then, you compare them to what you believe or know. There's a cross-pollination that can occur if it feels right. That's how people influence one another in a positive way. We are windows through which you can look. And if you see something you want, that other person has been a door opener for you. It's kind of exciting. I love meeting people. I treat each individual as my teacher. I ask, what can this person tell or show me that I need to know? Or this person has come into my life to see what I have and how it may change, grow or be erased from it. People are our best teachers, Colt. I truly believe that." Even her disastrous relationships had taught her about what to avoid in the next man.

"Well," he murmured, turning to Shelly, "you are an incredible teacher to me. I'm not so sure you need to learn from me, though. Your life has been filled with sunlight, mine with storms and darkness."

Shelly saw the somberness in his eyes, the heaviness in his roughened tone. "No life is all sunlight. I know that. I just wonder what might have been if your father hadn't guided you into your present career."

Colt hitched one shoulder and gestured toward the lake, now a deep turquoise because of the sunlight cascading down into this steep valley between the mountains. "When you talked about your passion, I remember as a little boy what excited me like that."

"What?"

"I liked walking the land. I would pick up a rock and feel the energy of it. And then, I'd touch a juniper trunk and talk to the spirit within it. A flower would feel different from the rock or the tree. I remember this incredible joy coming up through me." He made a gesture to his chest.

"That was passion you were feeling," she said.

"My father told me to stop picking up everything. He would take me back to the truck or the hogan to stop me from doing it. He'd tell me medicine men didn't do things like that. Instead, he'd teach me a song to sing."

"I see…"

Resting his hands on his hips, Colt scowled. "My passion, my love was in touching living things. I could touch a dog and know if it was sick or not. Or a horse. No matter what I put my hands on, I could pick up the energy and sensation from it, Shelly."

"In my paranormal experience, you sound like a natural for psychometry. A psychometrist is someone who can touch an object and pick up a vibe or feeling from it. Often, a visual picture, words or a complete scene will be given to you, as well."

"Yes." Colt stared at her. "That's what I used to be able to do."

"You still can," Shelly said. "That is another of your natural paranormal skills, Colt. All you have to do is allow it to come back. The right hemisphere of your brain is where all our skills resides. Just touch something, close your eyes and allow the information to flow into you. This is something you were born with and it won't disappear."

Turning, he said, "You mean to say that perhaps my path in life, my passion or skill, has nothing to do with me becoming a medicine man?" Even if that was true, Colt knew it would not make a difference. His path was to confront Yellow Teeth. And one of them would die.

Chapter 9

"They're doing the same thing," Victor snarled. He stood on the wooden deck of the busy teahouse that stood on one end of the lake. He watched the *Taqe* walk the banks of Agnes. Lothar and Jeff had binoculars and observed every step of their investigation. The one side of the lake was, for the most part, talus from the slopes above, although the evergreen trees grew down to the shore in places. For the most part it was easy to watch the *Taqe*.

"My lord, they are moving more slowly than they did at Lake Louise," Jeff said. "There are far more large boulders by the bank and they hesitate to check each set."

Grunting, Lothar said, "They seem particularly interested in any two that are together along the shore."

Victor scratched his head. "I have the fourth emerald sphere. It showed *me* the two boulders. How can *they* know one is white and the other black?"

"Do you think the sphere told the *Taqe* about them in a dream?" Lothar wondered.

"Anything is possible," Victor said with a scowl. "We didn't know that much about the spheres in the first place. We're learning as we go along. I thought it would only give information to me because now I'm its owner."

"Maybe they're hunting for a vortex where these boulders should be? Is that a combination that the sphere would be found in?" Jeff asked.

"It seems prudent to think in those terms," Victor said.

Lothar told Jeff to continue to watch the *Taqe* as they slowly made their way around the lake. "My lord, if that is so, then this is truly looking for a needle in a haystack. You've seen the topo map of this area. There are many lakes. If the *Taqe* don't know which lake, then they have an almost impossible job in front of them—just as we do."

Victor stepped off the deck and stood beneath a fir tree. Behind them stood the popular teahouse. There weren't many visitors at this time of morning, which suited him. "Well, if this is so," he told his underlings, "better they do the hard work and we just sit back and wait for them to find the sphere."

"Why would an Incan priest or priestess hide a sphere here in this area?" Jeff asked.

Grimacing, Victor snarled, "Who knows what was in the minds of those men and women Emperor Pachacuti sent out from Peru? They were to place them around the world in centers of power."

Lothar looked around the sunlight-drenched basin where Lake Agnes lay. "From a geomancy point of view," he said to no one in particular, "this is a place of great power." Lifting his finger, he pointed to the ring of mountains that surrounded the steep valley below. "We know mountains are a key energy, just as trees are. And when you have a circle of mountains like this that funnel into a narrow, small valley below, the power is much higher than it would be on a plain or set of low-lying hills."

"True," Victor said. "And if you look at Lake Louise, it's also in a similar design of mountains with a lake at the bottom of their massive slopes."

"Hmm," Victor said. He opened the topo map so it showed a part of their current area. "So, perhaps if they do not discover the sphere at Lake Agnes we would ask ourselves what other areas are similar to these two. That might be their next area to explore."

Lothar pointed to another oval lake. "My lord, the other possibility is Moraine Lake. It sits southeast

of Lake Louise and Lake Agnes. It, too, is surrounded by mountains just like this area."

"Interesting, interesting," Victor said. Excitement
wove through him. "We know they are looking for
a vortex, two boulders and a place of geomagnetic
power. They've already searched Lake Louise without finding the sphere. Now they've come to Lake
Agnes." Peering down the slope toward the turquoise lake, Victor said, "And if they don't find it
here, my bet is they'll go to Moraine Lake next."

"Do you want me or Jeff to go scout out Moraine
Lake while the *Taqe* are here?"

Considering the plan, Victor said, "Yes, go. This
lake is small and they will be done searching by
noon. I can watch. And if they find the emerald
sphere here, I can take it from them without your
help."

Jeff lowered his binoculars. He heard excitement
in the Dark Lord's tone. "It is a long hike over to
Moraine Lake. There is no easy way to reach it. We
need to go back down the trail to Lake Louise and
then drive over."

"Then get packing," Victor told them. "We'll be
in telepathic contact with one another. You let me
know when you get there. You'll have to stay over-
night at Moraine, so watch for grizzly bears over
there. This time of year they've just had their young
and are hungry. The elk and deer in this region have

also just had their babies and the grizzlies are looking for easy meat targets. Just stay alert."

Nodding, Jeff packed his binoculars away in the large pack he had on the ground near his feet. "My lord, just this morning a forest ranger put up a warning of bear activity on the trail at Moraine Lake."

"All the more reason to remain quick-witted," Victor growled.

Watching his men shrug into their large packs, Victor stood with the binoculars pressed against his eyes. His sense was that the emerald sphere was not at this lake. He couldn't be sure, however. Only when a *Taqe* got near enough to it would the emerald unveil its location. And it would never pop out of the fourth dimension to a *Tupay* like himself. Feeling impatient, Victor growled a curse as he watched the two work slowly and tediously along the rocky bank of the small lake.

"LOOK," SHELLY SAID, indicating an area about fifty feet ahead of them, "two boulders together."

Colt said, "I've never seen a lake with so many of the right-size boulders. Those two you see are both black. We need a black and a white one. Plus a vortex. And we haven't felt one of those yet."

"I know, I know," Shelly muttered, moving carefully along the talus. The stones were all rounded and therefore slippery. Her boots had good grip, but even so, it was dicey going. Holding out her arms to keep her balance, she worked her way along the bank toward the two boulders. "You're right. I haven't felt any vortex energy yet. And we're halfway around this lake." She stopped and straightened. The warmth of the morning sun felt good as it rose higher and higher into the sky. A golden eagle flew in lazy circles around the basin that contained the lake.

Colt came and stood nearby. He saw a sheen of perspiration on her face. He was sweating, too. "I would think this lake would have at least one." At this altitude trying to walk the bank was demanding. Sometimes, the rock slopes ended and there was a strip of yellowish-white soil. Colt was eager to get to those areas simply because they were easier to traverse. However, there were also relatively few boulders along the soil bank.

Pointing across the lake, Shelly said, "I'm sensing one over there."

Colt squinted his eyes and observed the area. Few people were at the lake yet. The water was like glass, the mountains above reflected dramatically in it. "Good, because I'm picking up on the same energy."

Shelly smiled at him. "We're a good team." She meant that in more than one way. As always, Colt was closed up and unreadable. Except to her. Now that she'd had the pleasure of seeing the rest of him, she could sense his emotions. Right now, the shadows in his narrowed eyes told her he wanted her. Mouth tingling in memory, Shelly understood as never before why they had to remain focused. She'd had a night to think about Yellow Teeth, his constant threat to Colt. And to herself. Colt would be unable to love anyone unless the Skin Walker was destroyed. How did one destroy a spirit? Shelly wanted to pursue that with him, but the time wasn't right.

"I don't see any physical signs that one could be over there," he said. "Trees that have five or more trunks or that bend or twist in a direction different from others show a vortex, too."

"I know. Sometimes, though, there are vortexes without any natural finger pointing at them." Shelly watched as Colt drank from his water bottle. *Look, but don't touch.* The rest of the way across the lake's bank, he'd remained in his introspective mode. Shelly could feel his turmoil. And, if her mind wasn't playing tricks on her, the turmoil was him wanting her in every possible way. *Oh, yes.* When she'd finally fallen asleep last night, her dreams had been torrid. Even now, she felt an ache deep within her. It was an ache only Colt could dissolve.

Sitting down on a large gray boulder near the shore, Shelly pulled out her water bottle and drank. At this high, dry altitude a person could get dehydrated and not even know it. Colt came and sat down on a boulder next to her. They'd been hunting relentlessly for nearly forty minutes. It was time to take a break.

Colt eased the pack off his back, opened it up and pulled out a health bar. "Want some?" he offered, peeling back the wrapper.

She nodded, capped her bottle and pushed it back into the net pocket on her pack. "Yes, it's time for a break." Slipping out of the knapsack, she set it down between them and sighed. "It feels good to sit down for a minute. My feet are killing me. Trying to stay upright on those slippery rounded stones is hard work."

"We need a little mountain goat in us," Colt said, a sour grin shadowing his mouth. He broke off half the protein bar and handed it to her. When their fingertips touched, he felt the doors to his pounding heart fly open. A moment didn't go by that he didn't think about Shelly in his arms—and in his bed. Nothing more than a fantasy, Colt realized. Frowning, he chewed on the grain bar and absorbed the beauty of the long oval lake.

"I've been thinking about your dream about a sorcerer," he told her.

"Oh?" Shelly bit into the bar.

Colt grimaced. "If this emerald sphere is so valuable and important, why didn't Yellow Teeth know about it before now?"

Stunned by the question, Shelly sat silent. Rubbing her brow, she said, "You're right. If he knew about it, why doesn't he know where it's located?"

Nodding, Colt absorbed her nearness. He enjoyed simply spending time and space with Shelly. "It doesn't make sense to me that Yellow Teeth is the sorcerer in your dream. Besides, if this emerald is important, that Skin Walker would have it already, and he'd have run off with it long before this. He's still around. I can feel him lurking at the edges of my energy protection."

A cold chill worked up Shelly's spine. "Every time you talk about him, I get a shiver." She rubbed her arms briskly. "If it isn't him, then who is it?"

"That is the question," Colt murmured, looking out across the lake and appreciating the dappled sunlight dancing across its turquoise surface. "Who else? I only know one kind of sorcery and that's the Skin Walker." He twisted his head and looked over at her. Shelly's brow was drawn down in thought and he could see the worry in her hazel eyes.

"Could we be being stalked by two types of sorcerers?" Shelly asked. It was so tough not to stare at Colt's mouth and vividly recall the strength of it upon her lips. "One known, one unknown?"

Shrugging, Colt muttered, "That's the conclusion I've come to."

"Would Yellow Teeth invite one of his witch friends to come here and be the second sorcerer?"

"No. They work alone. They fight among themselves, which is why they are loners." His mouth
flexed as he placed his arms around his knees. If he
didn't, he was going to reach out and place one
around Shelly's shoulders. "Remember Trip Nelson?"

"Yes."

"The strange energy around him? The stains in
his aura?"

"You didn't like him very much at all."

"It was more than that, Shelly. I felt threatened
by him. It was the same alarm that goes off deep
inside me if Yellow Teeth gets too close to me."

"Yet, you said he wasn't a Skin Walker." Shelly
sighed. "Nelson was different, but I didn't feel
threatened."

"That's because you have no training about the
dark or evil side."

She met his hooded eyes, felt the heat of her body
responding to that look. They might be talking about
evil, but Shelly felt nothing bad from Colt. There
was desire combined with raw need radiating off
him. He was hungry for her. Never had she been as
in touch with a man's energy as she was his. Shaken,
Shelly tried to set her feelings aside and think about
the threat. "I know I'm an idealist and all I know is
the soft and positive side of energy. I know bad
people are out there, Colt. I just don't know how to

pick up on them like you do." She gave him a sad look. "I wish I could. I know you're doing double duty with me around."

"I don't mind," Colt said. He saw Shelly's face grow red and he could feel her wanting to lean over and kiss him. Barely able to resist, he brutally reminded himself that Yellow Teeth would be waiting for just such an opening. He'd pounce like the coyote he was if Colt's focus was not on keeping the wall of energy strong.

For a moment, Shelly was entranced by the gleam in Colt's blue eyes. His pupils grew large. Her breath hitched. Oh, just to kiss him! Without thinking, she leaned forward just enough so that if he wanted to kiss her, he could. And if he didn't, he would pull away.

Groaning inwardly, Colt twisted around. The invitation was too much to resist! Sliding his hand around the curve of her neck, he brought Shelly fully into his arms. The warmth of the sun beat down upon them as his mouth sought her soft lips. This was a terrible risk, but in this moment of weakness, Colt became unabashedly human.

Breath catching, Shelly closed her eyes and sank into the strength and protection of Colt's arms. She felt his power, his mouth commanding hers, and she lost herself within the wild explosions that began deep in her lower body. Her breasts ached to be touched by him as he slid his mouth across hers. Nipples hardening against the wall of his chest, she slid her arms around his thick neck. His heartbeat raced in time with hers. His mouth plundered hers with a hunger she'd never encountered before. And yet, Shelly was equally starved for Colt's touch. His tongue moved tantalizing across her lower lip. She moaned, wanting more. Much more. His fingers threaded through her hair, massaging her scalp until she twisted against him, pleading for more. Shelly dissolved in pleasure she had not known until this moment, with this man.

When her mouth opened to allow him entrance, Colt felt as if he were falling into a cauldron of scalding heat that matched his own. Her tongue played languidly with his. Her breath was short and moist, matching his. As he moved his hand against her spine and pressed her breasts more firmly against his chest, he felt the puckered nipples. He moved his other hand down the slope of her shoulder, and his fingers grazed the curve of her breast. Shelly's moan was lost within him. Her softness felt so good as he explored the crescent beneath the fabric. His thumb and index finger settled around the nipple, and he heard her cry out in pleasure.

At that moment, Colt sensed what felt like a jet breaking the sound barrier right over him. Pleasure swirled with a warning. Every alarm in his body went off. *Yellow Teeth!*

Tearing his mouth from Shelly's, Colt pushed her away. Psychically, he saw the Skin Walker in coyote form coming out of the sky and charging directly at him. Still wrapped in the euphoria of pleasure and sexual need, Colt struggled to stand up. He had to stop the attack! As he twisted around, unsteady on the boulders, Colt heard Shelly give a cry of surprise. The splash of water followed. He couldn't turn to help her. He had to focus on the attack.

Yellow Teeth's coyote amber eyes narrowed upon him. The Skin Walker opened his mouth, his canines bared and dripping with saliva. He had only seconds to respond. To erect a barrier that would stop the Skin Walker from plowing into the top of his head and then taking over his body.

With a grunt, Colt threw up his hands. As he did, he visualized white light, like an unending wall that could not be penetrated. Would it be soon enough? Colt's fear overwhelmed his sensual needs. Yellow Teeth leaped at him, the coyote's legs with the claws extended and his teeth bared. Another blast of energy threw Colt off his feet. He landed with a groan as he slammed into the boulders and shallow water. Yellow Teeth hit the wall of energy and howled.

Colt opened his eyes as he struggled to sit up. The

witch had attacked the wall with a fury he'd never seen before. But it was too late! Colt watched as the coyote was flung back into another dimension. In seconds, the attack was over. Gasping for breath, Colt sat in the boulders and cold glacier-fed water realizing that he'd nearly been possessed.

Shelly gave a cry and lurched toward Colt. She dropped to her knees, not caring if she got wet as she gripped his shoulders.

"Colt! Are you all right?"

Hearing the terror in Shelly's voice snapped him back to the present. The wall had held, and they were both safe. Slowly getting up, he stood and gripped her arm. Her face was white with terror. "I'm okay. Are you?"

Shelly looked around. "What was that? What happened?"

"Yellow Teeth attacked," Colt told her grimly. He brought her into his arms and held her. She trembled like a little bird that had been tossed about during a violent storm. There had been a storm, all right, and the Skin Walker had damn near had him. If Colt hadn't torn his focus from Shelly, from their heated, exploring kiss, and answered the alarm, he'd be dead right now. Worse, Colt didn't want to think what would have happened to Shelly. Once a Skin Walker took over a body, he could live in it as long as he wanted. Shelly wouldn't realize what had happened.

And this all occurred because he'd been a slave to his body, to his need of her. It had nearly gotten them killed.

Stunned by the growl in Colt's tone, Shelly saw an icy coldness in his blue eyes. She felt murder around them. She felt Yellow Teeth's energy for the first time. "My God," she whispered, suddenly more afraid than ever before. "I didn't realize… I didn't…"

Colt held her and caressed her hair. "It's all right," he rasped. "He's gone. He can't hurt us now. We're safe."

Closing her eyes, Shelly simply held on to Colt. He was a bulwark of strength in a storm that frightened her. Just the gentle stroke of his hand across her hair calmed some of her anxiety. Pulling away, she searched his eyes. "Why did he attack now? I don't understand."

"Because I lost my focus on my shield that surrounds us," Colt explained. "I can't divide my awareness between you and him," he added. "It's one or the other, Shelly. I can't do both. And Yellow Teeth knew that. He took advantage of my lowered guard, that's all."

Shaking in earnest, Shelly whispered, "I put us in danger. I'm so sorry, Colt. I didn't know…" And she hadn't. But now she did. Seeing the turmoil in his eyes, she whispered, "Now I see why you're walled up. Why you can't be vulnerable. I understand." And it was heart-wrenching to realize the truth. Under no circumstances would Shelly ever put Colt into such a situation again. It would mean sitting on her feelings for him, not looking at him with that hunger. How was she going to do it? Shelly didn't have a ready answer, but after this attack, she had to try. She loved him too much to hurt him. Her love would be silent, never to be shared with him. Gathering her strength, Shelly pulled out of his arms. She was unsteady on her feet for a moment. After putting some distance between them, she held his frustrating gaze.

"I do understand," she said, her voice off-key.

Colt felt as if his heart were being ripped out of his chest. He saw the look on Shelly's face, the dawning awareness of what he lived with every day of his life. Her love for him shone in her hazel eyes, never to be expressed toward him. Bitterness, grief and loss assailed him as he stood there breathing hard, his arms empty, his chest with a hole in it. "Now you do," was all he could manage.

Gazing around at the placid scene, Shelly suddenly felt old and tired. Even though Yellow Teeth's attack had been thwarted at the last moment, the residual evil energy was sucking life out of her. Closing her eyes, she stopped the loss of energy by visualizing an oblong globe of white and gold light surrounding her, head to toe. The tiredness stopped, and balance restored. She could taste the evil of Yellow Teeth in her mouth. She could smell the carrion odor that had come with him. Once she opened her eyes, she saw that Colt was in complete control once more. His face was expressionless, his shield impenetrable. He was the warrior he'd always been. Yet Shelly sensed deep grief over what had happened. He'd never said, *I love you.* Colt didn't have to. Shelly had felt the man's unbridled love with that kiss that had rocked her out of this world.

She forced herself to move to the shore. Once there, she turned and saw Colt coming across the boulders toward her. When he leaped the last few feet to the pebbly shore and stood next to her, Shelly wanted to cry.

"I'm sorry," Colt murmured, turning to her and seeing the tears glistening in her eyes. He felt her heart and her love and the grief all rolled into one. Colt placed his hand on her shoulder for a moment. He absorbed her closeness, her unspoken love for him. The spicy scent of her hair, the touch of her cheek against his, soothed his chaotic emotions. "I have dreams," he told her in a low tone. *Dreams of you.* But he didn't dare mouth those words. Colt saw how many obstacles were in his way. "I believe dreams can come true someday. I want you to hold on to that, Shelly."

His raspy words tore at her. "Then I'll dream the

same dream you do." His energy felt as if he were on some invisible precipice. His eyes clearly showed his anguish, and yet hope burned deep within them. Hope for a life of freedom where he could be rid of the evil that stalked him and could walk a new path—with her at his side.

Without a word, Shelly stepped forward and threw her arms around his shoulders. His arms swept strongly around her and he crushed her to him. Colt buried his face next to hers and she felt the pounding of his heart against her own. Closing her eyes, she whispered, "We'll get through this together. I promise…"

Chapter 10

"What the hell were you thinking?" Victor roared at Yellow Teeth. He'd felt the attack by the Skin Walker on the male *Taqe* and could barely contain his rage. He'd hauled the shape-shifter back to the *Tupay* fortress.

"It's my right to go after him!" Yellow Teeth snarled. "His walls were finally down! Do you know how long I've been waiting for that to happen?"

Balling his fist, Victor glared across the desk at the arrogant Skin Walker. "You've a lot to learn, Yellow Teeth. You're under my direction and orders." He rose and bared his teeth as he leaned forward. "You never disobey an order I give you. There's a reason why I gave it, you stupid idiot!"

Smugly, Yellow Teeth shook his head. "This is a vendetta. My revenge."

"I don't care!" Victor shouted, his voice rolling like thunder around the office. The very walls trembled in the wake of his anger. Yellow Teeth's thick eyebrows suddenly rose. Victor had unveiled five percent of the power that he owned and blasted the Skin Walker. It had hurled the shape-shifter into the door. When the spirit fell to his knees, shock registered in his expression.

"It appears that your kind needs a lot more discipline," Victor rasped as he came around the desk and put his face into the Skin Walker's. "From this day forward, all Skin Walkers are going to be coming back to basic-training school here at the *Tupay* fortress every week!"

"But…"

"Shut up!" Victor shouted at him, spittle flying out of his mouth and upon the man's tense face. "You're under my command! You'd better get it, Yellow Teeth. If you don't, I have the capacity to once and for all destroy your soul."

Eyes widening, Yellow Teeth leaned back as the rage of the Dark Lord finally penetrated his arrogance and confidence. Staring up into the fathomless black eyes of Victor Carancho Guerra, he got it. "Y-yes, my lord. I—I won't do that again."

Straightening, Victor walked back to his desk and sat down. "Damn you. You've compromised our ability to track this couple. All because you want revenge, you defied my orders."

Scrambling to his feet, Yellow Teeth opened his hands and walked to the desk. "Please, my lord, don't send me away! I promise, I'll wait until you tell me it's time to kill Colt Black. I killed his sister. Surely, you'll let me kill him? His father killed my body. I want this revenge."

Victor glowered at him. "Not over the importance of this mission, you dolt! My knights are trained not to give in to human emotions. They are the best of the best here in the world of the *Tupay*. In comparison to them, you are a child spirit. You have no discipline. No greater understanding of anything outside yourself!" Shaking his index finger at Yellow Teeth, he said, "Do you realize how important this mission is? Do you even understand the emerald sphere and what it can mean to all of us? No, you don't. And you don't care because all you want is your stupid revenge." Snorting, Victor glared at the stricken Skin Walker. "Your kind has had it too easy. You need to train up to the understanding you're not out there operating alone and free to do what you want on a whim. My spirits and humans need discipline. It's the only way we hold the fabric of what we control in spirit and on Earth with human beings. Our whole focus is destroying the Warriors for the Light. Anyone with a Vesica Pisces birthmark is marked for death—by us." He jabbed his thumb into his own chest.

Wiping his mouth, Yellow Teeth tried a simpering smile. His canines showed and saliva dribbled from the corners of his mouth. "My lord," he pleaded, opening his hands in supplication, "please, please allow me to remain with your team. I promise," he said, pressing his hand against his heart, "to remain far away. I promise to come only when you tell me to come to attack the *Taqe*. I swear upon my soul, I will never disobey another order from you." Giving the Dark Lord a pleading look, Yellow Teeth got down on his knees before him. "I beg of you, my lord, allow me this."

Victor stood glaring down at the whining shapeshifter. "I ought to kill you myself." The words hung like ice in the tension of the room. Yellow Teeth's eyes widened tremendously. Chastened, he allowed his hands to fall to his sides and remained in a kneeling position before the Dark Lord. "I am yours to do with as you please, my lord." He hung his head.

Not for an instant did Victor think that Yellow Teeth possessed this instant humility. No, he saw the

Skin Walker's aura and knew it was all a game with him. He was familiar with coyote energy. They were the tricksters of the North American continent. Studying the bowed head of the Skin Walker, Victor's mind whirled with options.

He knew Yellow Teeth was highly regarded among the Skin Walker clan. It would do the clan good to see the stupid idiot killed. But then, Yellow Teeth had come to him with the information that had put them on the trail of the *Taqe* looking for the next emerald sphere. If Victor killed him, the word would go out that such loyalty was not rewarded. He couldn't risk that happening. But this idiot didn't need to know his thoughts or manipulations.

"Do I have your promise on your soul that you will obey every order I give you?" Victor thundered at him.

Snapping his head up, Yellow Teeth cried, "Oh, yes, my lord! I promise upon my soul!" He clasped both hands to his heart as he gave the Dark Lord a beseeching look.

Inwardly, Victor laughed to himself. This witch was so low on the totem pole of energy it was laughable. But Victor needed the bastard. He saw the man's brown eyes widen as he begged for a second chance. "Very well, Yellow Teeth. You're still on our team. You are to distance yourself so that this *Taqe* you attacked will not even feel you around. You got that? You've attacked him and now he's really on guard. You've made our work ten times harder."

"And I'm sorry for that, my lord," Yellow Teeth whined. He tried to smile. "I promise, I shall remain out of sight and sensing of this *Taqe*. I will redeem myself in your eyes."

Victor doubted that, but he might have need of a fourth *Tupay* to steal the emerald sphere when it was found. "Very well. Get up!" He made a sharp gesture for the witch to rise to his feet.

Yellow Teeth leaped upward and started forward to touch the Dark Lord.

"Don't you dare touch me!" Victor snarled.

Chastened, Yellow Teeth quickly stepped away. "Yes, my lord. I'm sorry, my lord."

Convinced that Yellow Teeth understood greater power, Victor jerked open the door. "Get out of here. Go back down there with my team and telepathically tell them your orders. And then, lie in wait like a good coyote always does."

"Yes, my lord," Yellow Teeth whispered, smiling with glee. "That I can do!"

Victor stood in the doorway of his office and watched the witch blink out of *their* dimension. Turning, he shut the door, deep in thought. What to do now? The male *Taqe* was clearly on guard. Worse, the *Taqe* had easily stopped the witch's attack. Clearly, he was a Warrior for the Light, not the usual *Taqe* individual. The fact troubled Victor even more. It had been one thing to take the sphere from the last couple since neither had been a Warrior. This time around, the male was a Warrior; therefore his power could be almost equal to Victor's. Colt Black was an unknown energy.

Rubbing his chin, Victor paced his office, devising a strategy that would undermine the *Taqe* team without their knowledge. Damn Yellow Teeth! He'd thrown a wrench into his plans. This witch had a powerful energy, and it had bounced harmlessly off Black's aura. That was real power and Victor knew it. If push came to shove, Victor would send Yellow Teeth into the fray at the right moment to attack the Warrior. If Black destroyed the witch, it was no matter to Victor. The death would open an avenue for him to go in and possess the Warrior for the Light. It might be the only way. He would sacrifice Yellow Teeth to lower Black's energy level and once his shield was down, Victor would strike.

Victor halted and frowned. Yes, Yellow Teeth was going to pay for his revenge. He would have his soul destroyed once and for all by the very man he wanted revenge from. Well, that was his lot in the cosmos, Victor decided. Some spirits gave their lives for the improvement of the whole *Tupay* empire. Smiling a little, Victor congratulated himself on his new plan. The witch had caused all of this and would soon fix it. It was a just reward for Yellow Teeth usurping his authority. Cosmic karma at its best. Victor continued to ponder Colt Black's power. The woman's energy was weak in comparison. He could tell by simply looking at her aura that she was not a Warrior for the Light. Just a normal run-of-the-mill *Taqe*.

Victor recalled his own daughter, Ana, who had nearly killed his soul when he'd attacked Mason, the man she loved. Mason was a Warrior for the Light, too. And Victor had had him beaten down and nearly killed until his daughter waded into the fray. She had sent him love, the one human emotion he could not deal with. And if he'd allowed her love for Mason to touch him, Victor's soul would be dead and gone. Victor hoped Colt Black wasn't able to send love at him. If so, it could kill Victor.

Black didn't seem very loving, almost the opposite. Everything about the man's aura, what little Victor could perceive of it, shouted *Warrior*. Well, he'd have to take that chance. Or maybe he would send Lothar to possess him. Better to lose a knight than his own life. He'd just have to see what should be done if they found the emerald sphere at that moment.

Since there was little else he could do, Victor willed himself back into Trip Nelson's body and joined the rest of his team. Lothar and Jeff were hidden in a stand of woods, looking down. The attack by Yellow Teeth had just happened. Turning when he appeared before them, Lothar handed him a pair of binoculars.

"They're shaken up, my lord," he said.

"I'm sure they are."

"Yellow Teeth really screwed us," Lothar muttered, frowning.

"I know. I've had a talk with him."

"Yes, he already told us." Lothar shook his head. "He's done us a lot of damage, my lord."

Victor could see in his knight's eyes the question: Why had he allowed the shape-shifter back among them? He didn't have time to explain his strategy to his knight.

"We'll recover." Victor sat on a fallen log with the binoculars pressed to his eyes. So, the *Taqe* were down there embracing one another. *How sweet.* The last team had fallen in love and weren't watching their backs as they should. A thrill moved through him and he smiled. This was an excellent development that left them some options. If Black allowed his love for the woman to trump his ability to stay on guard, they had another opening. Just what Victor wanted.

He had to be more careful this time. Both *Taqe* were clairvoyant. However, they didn't sense him in the possessed body he wore. Being in Trip Nelson's body was a distinct advantage. The male *Taqe* did not trust Trip so Victor could not blithely walk back into their lives, pretend to be a guide and work with them from that vantage point. The woman was very gullible, Victor thought with a slight grin. Plus, neither knew that Jeff and Lothar had possessed the bodies of the twins. They were his secret weapons if he had to use one to get the sphere.

He watched the man and woman separate from their embrace. If he sent a telepathic energy line to hook into them, Black would feel it in a heartbeat. Victor wanted to know what they were saying to one another but contented himself with simply watching.

"ARE YOU OKAY?" Shelly asked Colt, her voice shaking. As they separated from their embrace, she felt his shields come up, his face becoming unreadable.

"I'm fine." Colt looked around. The day was beautiful. Yet he'd nearly lost his life to the witch. He glanced over at Shelly, who still seemed shocked by everything that had happened. Of course, anyone would be. Yellow Teeth's power wasn't to be trifled with. Colt wondered where the bastard was now and sent out feelers with no success. Had their confrontation injured the spirit of the witch? Colt had no way to know.

"Will he attack us again?" Shelly quavered.

"I don't know. I don't feel him anywhere near us right now."

Rubbing her arms as she sat on the boulder, her clothes wet, she whispered, "My God, Colt, I've never experienced anything like this. You warned me about him. I believed you." She bit down on her lower lip. "But now I understand. I really do." She studied him with new respect. "You're right—I'm a real liability. If you hadn't been here…"

"Don't go there," Colt warned her. "Yellow Teeth is after me, not you." That was a lie, but looking at Shelly, he couldn't afford to tell her the unvarnished truth. The Skin Walker would take her out to get even with him. That's how a coyote shape-shifter worked: take out the victims and make their survivors, their loved ones, suffer in grief. Flexing his fingers, Colt desperately wanted to wrap his hands around that son of a bitch's neck and kill him. He wanted Yellow Teeth's soul. If the witch was stupid enough to engage him directly, then a battle for total victory would follow. His rage over Mary's death, and now this attack, would fuel his passion to send the witch away forever. Yellow Teeth did not have that same passion behind the attack. All he had was selfish desire and that was nothing up against Colt's emotional storm. This might make all the difference in a life-and-death battle.

"How are you feeling?" he asked Shelly. How he

wished he could hold her, but he couldn't take that chance again. No matter how much he was falling in love with Shelly, he could never show it to her. No more kisses. No more embraces. The prospect felt like a knife serrating his heart into a million bleeding pieces.

"I'm a little shaky," she admitted with a half laugh. "Wow, it happened so fast. I didn't feel him coming at us until it was too late."

Colt got up and held out his hand to her. They were both wet from the attack. "Let's continue our search around the lake. It's better to focus on something positive."

Holding out her hand, Shelly grasped his. After Colt pulled her to her feet and helped her to the pebbled shore, he released her. It was all she would have of Colt from now on. Shelly tried to redirect her grief and focus on why they were here.

"Do you think Yellow Teeth will hit us again?"

Shrugging, Colt said, "I don't know. But we can't live in fear of him. I never have and I'm not going to start now."

"You're fearless," Shelly said, admiration in her tone. Girding herself, she visualized roots from her feet sinking deep into the Earth. It would help ground her.

Giving her a slight smile, Colt said, "Skin Walkers feed off our fear. I can't live in fear of that bastard."

Then he had a lot to feed off her, Shelly thought, but she only nodded and said nothing. Colt needed her to be brave regardless of the churning tightness in her gut. "Let's go. Let's finish checking out this lake."

They continued to hunt along the edge of the lake, going about a thousand feet around the shore when Colt said, "I feel a vortex."

Shelly walked across the precarious rocky ground on the bank of the lake where Colt stood. "You're good. I didn't feel anything."

"You're still in shock over the attack, that's all. By tomorrow morning you'll be able to feel vortexes again." Peering ahead in the sunlight, Colt was glad he had a baseball cap on, as the bill shaded his eyes against the sunlight. "There are a lot of boulders up ahead, too, where I'm feeling that energy."

Shelly nodded. "Maybe we'll get lucky," she said a little breathlessly, slipping and sliding on the talus as they made their way forward. "I see a lot of rocks."

"We've got to have the right combo—a black and a white boulder sitting together along with a vortex."

"The vortex is a small one," she said.

"Yes."

"It's what I call a neutral or an androgynous energy. That means this vortex funnels male and female energy. It's complete or whole."

Colt held Shelly's hand as she slipped and nearly fell on the smooth stones beneath their booted feet. "Take it easy. It's not going anywhere," he teased. Colt understood she was trying to be of help even though some of her clairvoyant abilities were off-line. He tried another tack to keep her involved and feeling as if she were needed.

"On the Navajo reservation, the androgynous vortexes have their own schedule to go on- and off-line. They serve different and highly unique functions for Mother Earth. We consider them whole or perfect because they have combined their male and female energies. Their job description is unique—vortexes have either male or female energy."

Shelly stood next to Colt. It was a special hell not to reach out and hold his hand or lean against his strong body. "I've found androgynous vortexes can take on a particular need for a local or regional area."

"It's true. They play different parts in given areas of Mother Earth's body. They can be portals."

"Yes, I've experienced that with these types of vortexes, too." She was glad his experience was equal to hers.

"Exactly," Colt praised, giving her a look of pride. Now that Shelly was focused on vortex-hunting, her face was no longer pale. Her eyes were losing their shocked look, as well. "On this planet, there are doors to other places and other dimensions. It may be to another planet in this solar system, another star, a galaxy or somewhere else in the universe. Or they can be an opening or doorway to another dimension. It can be the past, somewhere in our present or the future."

"I've found that to be true no matter where I've gone in the world," Shelly agreed.

Colt stared critically at the area where he knew the vortex was located. They were on the very fringes of it. "In Navajo stories, it is said that in certain mesas there are openings for the Anasazi people to come and go into our world. I've heard the old medicine men discuss this and I've been taken to these portals." Colt shook his head. "Archeologists know that the Anasazi people lived where the Navajo now live. And they all agree that the Anasazi suddenly disappeared without a trace. They don't know where they went. Our stories say they left this world through a door in a mesa that goes to another world."

"And have you gone through one of those portals?" Shelly asked, holding his hooded gaze.

"No. I wasn't allowed. Only the oldest of the elders makes a trip through that particular portal to talk with the elders on the other side."

"That's fascinating," Shelly said. "I've gone through some. One was in Scotland near the Roslyn Chapel just outside Edinburgh. The vortex took me back to the Templars in southern France. It was a doorway to that particular century and place."

"There's another story, too," Colt said, watching as color seeped back into her cheeks. "Many of them claim to have spoken with aliens from other star systems. They have said that there is another mesa with a door through which these aliens come and go between our world and theirs. These aliens, we refer to them as 'star people,' have had continuing conversations with our elder medicine people."

"That's mind-blowing!" Shelly said. "An androgynous vortex is a door to someone, another dimension, age, place and space. You've heard of the parallel-universe theory?"

"Yes," he said, "we had a science teacher in high school who was very excited about the possibility. I found it interesting because I had known about these doors in the mesas. I remembered sitting with my father many times with the elder medicine men and they would discuss these star people."

"If people really knew what was around them," Shelly began. She felt Colt's smile rather than seeing it. Just being with him made her feel protected.

"I'm going to move into the vortex," he told her. "You stay here. Right now, your aura isn't balanced and you're not ready to deal with it."

Becoming serious, Shelly nodded. "You're right. But be careful, Colt."

As he approached the area, he felt suddenly dizzy. He knew it was his aura adjusting to the higher frequency and whirling motion of the vortex. Once the dizziness passed, he moved forward. Eyes narrowed, Colt looked for the two special boulders. There were plenty around, but not the ones he was seeking. Halting, he saw no reason to move any deeper into the vortex. In order to know where it led, he'd have to step completely into its energy. Given he'd been attacked and his energy wasn't where it needed to be, Colt decided to be cautious.

Once free of the energy, he turned and looked at Shelly, whose eyes were wide with worry. "The boulders we need aren't there. I'm not going any farther."

"Good," Shelly whispered as she saw him walk back toward her. "Can we walk around it?"

Nodding, Colt stopped his hand from coming forward to cup her elbow to help her up and around the area. "Yes. Just follow me." Colt stepped across the talus with care. The slope ended and then they were back on the yellow earth. Grass and flowers grew along the bank where the soil reached the glacial lake. The sun was higher and the temperature was on the rise. Colt took off his jacket and carried it as they plodded along. There was nothing along the last part of this lake and he looked forward to walking around the end to the teahouse.

Finally, they were back on the trail that would lead to a helicopter landing pad near the lake and then to the house. Colt followed Shelly, watching the sun touch her shoulder-length hair. She wore a baseball cap but the breeze lifted strands across her shoulders. Her hair was magical, like her, Colt decided. The copper blazed red and the breeze revealed burgundy and gold within. He hotly re-membered touching those silky tresses. He wanted to do it again. But then grief rolled in and snuffed out all his needs.

Colt couldn't shake the feeling they were being watched once again and tried to ferret out the energy. It wasn't Yellow Teeth's energy signature. No, this was that other energy he'd picked up on a few days ago. Was it the other sorcerer, the unknown and unnamed one? Knowing the other sorcerer was near and keeping tabs on them made him edgy. More than anything, Colt wanted to keep Shelly safe. As they finished their investigation of the bank and began the long climb up the slope to the teahouse, Colt promised himself that the unknown sorcerer would never harm her. Not ever.

Chapter 11

Colt and Shelly got their hot coffee and bakery goods at the busy teahouse, then set out to find a place out in the sun to enjoy it. They settled down next to one another on a bank, coffee in hand, and spread the topo map out in front of them.

"Mmm, good coffee," Shelly said, absorbing Colt's closeness. "I needed this to calm my nerves." The sun was strong and soothing as it lifted the coolness of the morning. The teahouse sat at the top of the steep trail that led down to Lake Agnes. It was a large log and stone structure, and she appreciated the many-colored, smooth granite stones used to create the foundation. The odors of fresh pastries being baked did nothing but add to the magic of the morning. She smelled split pea soup with ham, too. After the terrible attack by Yellow Teeth, she was ready for some quiet time.

"It is," Colt said, relishing his black coffee. His alertness remained on high because he didn't believe Yellow Teeth would remain away for long. Had the Skin Walker been injured? Colt hoped so. In his heart, he knew that soon, he would have to deal with the witch once and for all.

For a brief moment, their knees touched. Colt relished the sensation but reluctantly moved away. Sometime in the future—if he survived—they might be able to show their feelings, but not now. The incredible turquoise color of Lake Agnes made it look like a sparkling gemstone set in the grayish-colored brooch of the surrounding mountains. Shelly had taken off her baseball cap and her shoulder-length red hair was a frame for her pale skin and copper freckles. She was beautiful.

"Did you feel the energy shift after we came out of the teahouse?" he asked her, his brows drawing downward.

"Yes. What do you make of it?" Shelly asked.

"When we got close to the building, I felt a pressure in my chest. When I get that, it's a warning of an evil spirit nearby. I turned on my clairvoyance and looked around and couldn't see anything wrong in the auras of the people around us."

"Do you think it was Yellow Teeth?"

"No, it's the other sorcerer you picked up on in your dream. The one we can't identify—yet." Shaking his head, Colt could feel someone watching from a distance. "We have two threats," he told her in a low tone. "We know who one is. The other, we don't. And that leaves us vulnerable." He didn't say that he was more worried for Shelly than for himself.

"A sorcerer in spirit or in human form?"

Colt shrugged. "I wish I knew."

"Or a sorcerer in spirit like Yellow Teeth who has possessed a human body to track us?"

"That's possible, too." He stared at the beauty of the lake before them. "I just don't know. And it's eating me alive."

"We agree that Trip Nelson was suspicious," Shelly said, giving him a glance. Colt's face was hard and unreadable. "For what it's worth, I feel that he's a wolf in sheep's clothing. That's all I sense. I wish I had more of an impression."

"I'd bet money that the other sorcerer has possessed Nelson's body, but I don't know for sure." Looking up the flower-strewn trail that led to the teahouse, he added, "At least fifty people are around the teahouse area. It's impossible to look at the auras of every one of them. My ability has its limits. I scanned the ones I saw coming up the trail earlier, but no red flags went up."

Nodding, Shelly said, "Same for me. I was feeling like we were being watched. The people I saw weren't looking at us. And like you, I have limited energy and ability to look at auras. I have to shift into an altered state and then look at them. My energy can hold up for a little while, but after that, I have to sleep in order to recharge my psychic batteries. It sounds like it's the same for you."

"Exactly," Colt said. He glanced up at the teahouse. It was overflowing with people. Some were sitting outside or were perched on the broad wooden steps that led up to the popular place. The chatting could be heard even down where they sat in the lush grass. "I feel him around but I don't know which one he is." His gut was tight, almost painful. The adrenaline from the earlier attack was still within his bloodstream and he felt as if someone had stuck a hundred needles into him.

"Same here."

"Well," Colt said, giving her a worried look, "it means one thing—the unnamed sorcerer is here and he's waiting while we try to find that emerald."

A shiver passed through Shelly. Nodding, she sipped her coffee. The raspberry danish in her lap suddenly didn't seem as luscious and her appetite fled. "You're right." The attack had left her shaken to her core. Could she handle another one? Fear of dying was real to Shelly as never before.

While he wanted to reach out and console her, Colt didn't. "We have to stay alert, Shelly. We can't get caught off guard." His voice grew deep with concern. "I like what we share, but we can't let it interfere with our focus. Not until…well…" Colt's voice trailed off. There was no sense in making her even more scared than she was already.

"You're right, Colt." She managed a smile. "It's tough ignoring you." Shelly ached to tell Colt she was falling in love with him, but that would only hurt them both. "The fear of possession is scary, Colt. This emerald's a lot more important than we first realized."

Colt finished off his coffee and set the empty cup next to his day pack. Flattening his hands, he smoothed out the topo map. "It is. But why? We know so little about it," he growled. "Here is the Lake Louise road. We can trek back to the hotel and then drive over to Moraine Lake. There's a lodge and a nice trail that runs along the north shore of the lake. The trail ends near a stream that comes from the Wenkchemna Glacier. That means walking the shoreline on our own again."

"Probably fighting a lot of talus, slipping and sliding around," Shelly griped. "I wonder if they have canoes to rent at that lodge. It would be a lot easier to check the shoreline that way."

Colt said, "Great idea. When we drive over, we'll go find out. I'd rather paddle than fight steep, rocky terrain." He closed the map and placed it back into a net pocket on the side of his nylon day pack. Looking up the slope, he saw a number of hikers sitting on the edge of the lake enjoying the morning sunshine.

"Do you think we might find those two boulders at Moraine Lake?" Colt asked her. Shelly licked the raspberry jam off her fingers. The act was innocent but it filled him with a fierce desire to capture her hands and close his mouth upon her glistening lips. Never having experienced such powerful urges before, Colt began to realize how much he had to restrain himself.

"I hope so," she said, finishing off the danish. "Our dreams showed a rounded shore of an oval lake. We have plenty of oval lakes in this area. I wish our dreams could have been more specific."

Settling back on his elbows, the sunlight warming him, Colt closed his eyes. Right now, he didn't feel the sorcerer as he had before. Maybe he had backed off or disappeared among the many hikers. "There's worse things to do," he said. How badly Colt wished they were alone in this lovely hollow where the flowers along the banks of Agnes reminded him of a rainbow. He'd like nothing more than to pull Shelly into his arms, kiss her hotly and undress her.

They could make beautiful love here heated by the sun and held in the embrace of the raw, stunning landscape that surrounded them. His dreams were just that and Colt gently tucked them away.

Shelly pulled her pack into her lap and opened it up. "Oh, no disagreement! I love hiking. And Banff is incredibly gorgeous. The color in these lakes makes them seem more magic than real." She sighed. "Besides, I have this terribly handsome partner who I think the world of at my side. How good can life get?" It was forced gaiety. Shelly didn't want to sink into the fear that ate at her.

The pink flush on her cheeks made her freckles stand out even more. Colt reined in his wild desires that clamored for attention. He remembered the dream's warning that the unknown sorcerer would kill them if they found the emerald. "My life has become interesting since I met you," he murmured.

"What an effect to have on people," Shelly said, meeting his burning gaze that told her how much he wanted her. Bringing the hood down on her pack, she closed it and put it aside. Rising, she said, "I'll be back."

Watching her walk on the trail toward the tea-house, her hips swaying, Colt inhaled raggedly. This was a special hell for him. Never had he been so drawn to a woman before and there were two sorcerers tracking them. Grimly, he sat up and put his arms around his drawn-up knees. As always, he watched the people coming and going on the trail to the teahouse. It was just habit.

"WELL?" VICTOR GROWLED at Lothar and Jeff, who stood with him on the trail to the teahouse. "What do you think?"

Lothar put down the binoculars. "He's onto us, I think."

"He doesn't have a clue who we are," Victor snorted. "He's probably prickly because of Yellow Teeth's assault this morning. Our cover is still intact."

Jeff frowned and moved to the side of the Dark Lord. "He's powerful, isn't he?"

Nodding, Victor cut a glance to Jeff. "Yes, any Warrior for the Light is. Now, you're getting a first-hand taste of one in action. You saw what he did to that witch."

"I've never met one until now," Jeff admitted, watching the Navajo medicine man on the slope. "They can kill us?"

"Of course they can!" Lothar yelled. "You should know that from your schooling."

"I do, Lothar. But listening to stories and having a teacher tell you a Warrior for the Light is dangerous is one thing." He motioned to the Native American. "Seeing one in action is a different experience."

Victor held up his hand. "Not all Warriors for the Light have the same skills. They are all unique in their abilities, just as we are. For example, I'm not very knowledgeable about vortexes, but Lothar is."

"So," Jeff began with a frown, "we can't really know what a particular *Taqe*'s abilities are until we meet them in combat?"

"Exactly," Victor grumbled. "And given that Black was fully engaged with his beloved little red-haired bitch when Yellow Teeth attacked him and he was still able to fend him off, that tells me a lot."

Jeff gave the Dark Lord a searching look. "What does it tell you? I don't understand the significance."

Lothar sighed and gave Victor a shake of his head. "Trainees," he muttered.

Jeff smiled a little at the knight whose frustration was etched on his features. "How else am I to learn? Schooling is important but being out on a mission is much more exciting and educational for me."

"That's why you're along," Victor said. "You had the highest marks upon graduation. A student like you should be in the field at every opportunity available to you." Victor cast Lothar a disparaging glance. "And I know you don't like fledgling trainees, but Jeff is up to this task."

"Yes, my lord," Lothar said in a respectful tone. "You are right, as always."

"To answer your question," Victor said, watching

Black through the binoculars once more, "this particular Warrior has a lot of power. More than most that I've met in combat."

"How does that translate for us?" Jeff wondered, relieved that the Dark Lord didn't mind his training-wheels presence.

Taking the binoculars away from his eyes, Victor noted a group of hikers coming by and waited. Once they were out of earshot, he said, "Black was completely focused on the woman. Normally, when your focus is elsewhere, there is an automatic opening in your aura where we can take advantage. Yellow Teeth is not a weak witch energetically speaking. He's one of the most powerful Skin Walkers on the Navajo reservation. For him to strike Black with all his power and to have Black respond and protect himself and the woman tells me he's on the top rung."

"Rung of what?" Jeff asked.

"Strength of spirit is gained by hundreds and thousands of lifetimes. The more strength you have, the more powerful you become."

Lothar stepped onto the trail and nailed Jeff with a look. "The Dark Lord has been alive and in and out of human form for four thousand years. And before that, he had one hundred thousand lifetimes here on Earth and in other dimensions before he ever took over that position." Lothar gestured into

the air. "Energy is gained through living incarnations. Since your last lifetime was during World War
Two, you understand the principles of a power
station?"

Jeff nodded. "Yes, I do."

Pleased, Lothar said, "You're aware of the
Hoover Dam?"

"Of course."

"All right," he said, "the Dark Lord is that powerful. We, in comparison, can be seen as electrical
substations of varying power or wattage."

Jeff regarded Victor with new respect. "That's
incredible."

"Yes," Victor said, pleased. "I am powerful." He
jabbed his finger at Black. "But this Warrior is more
than just a substation, so to speak."

"So," Jeff grappled, "you can't really know how
powerful he is until you personally engage him in
energy combat?"

"Exactly," Victor said.

"But," Jeff said, opening his hands, "are there
any *Taqe* who are like Hoover Dam?"

Grimacing, Victor said, "Yes. At the *Taqe* stronghold, the Village of the Clouds, their leaders, Adaire
and Alaria, are equal to me in authority and power.
They had at least a hundred thousand lifetimes as
Druids all over Europe before they were both killed
at Mona Island by the Roman soldiers. From that

time on, they were elevated to this status as spiritual leaders of the *Taqe* nation."

"The great mother goddess of us all has decreed that each side shall have equal power," Lothar said.

"Why?"

Shrugging, Lothar said, "That's just the way it is."

Jeff stared at Black for a long time before turning back to his master. "What could possibly defeat you?"

"The one thing that can drive me or any *Tupay* off is the energy of love," Victor said uneasily.

"Yes, I'd been taught that," Jeff said. "It just seems weird to me. Why love?"

Lothar rolled his eyes. "Everything about the *Tupay* is about getting what we want. That is not love. In the goddess's eyes, love is the greatest power in the universe."

"So, love really does conquer all?" Jeff asked.

"It can," Victor said unhappily. "But there's a fly in that ointment, too."

"Oh?" Jeff said.

"While being attacked, it's very hard for anyone to be able to love the attacker," Victor said, grinning a little. "Could you have loved your enemies who killed you in World War Two?"

Jeff scowled. "Of course not. I have hatred and anger. I'd like to find them either in body or spirit and get back what they took from me. If I had lived, I'd have spent the rest of my life with my family. I'd have watched my children grow up and have their children."

"Exactly," Victor said, triumphant. He waggled his finger at Black. "So, the real question about him is this—can Black resurrect love instead of rage or hatred toward us if we attack him?"

Rubbing his chin, Jeff studied Black. "I see. And you won't know until you're in the act of possession?"

"Precisely," Victor told him.

"And if he can?"

"We'll break off the attack and get the hell back to the *Tupay* fortress."

"But if he can, why couldn't this Warrior come to the *Tupay* fortress and send his love to each and every one of us?"

"Because it simply can't be done," Lothar said. "Adaire and Alaria, who are the leaders of the *Taqe*, have the capacity to do this to a few of us, but certainly not all of us. In reality, there are simply too many of us and sooner or later, they, too, will run out of energy. It's always been a stalemate between the heavy and light energy forces."

"So, it's a true stalemate," Jeff concluded. "We have to take out the *Taqe* one at a time just as they are focused on us."

Victor laughed. "Now you're getting it, my boy.

We're only at risk on an individual basis if a Warrior or any *Taqe* can send us love instead of fear, anger or hate when we attack them."

"But if we are caught by love," Jeff persisted, "then, as I understand from my classroom training, we either have to turn into a *Taqe* or our soul dies. And if it dies, we are no more—forever."

"That's right. Turn and be a traitor to your own kind or die a permanent death," Lothar said.

The bitter taste in Jeff's mouth made him wrinkle his nose. "That's a helluva choice."

Shrugging, Victor said, "Don't worry. Not many have had to make that choice in our history."

"Those that did," Jeff asked, "did they die or turn into a *Taqe?*"

"They've all died," Lothar said proudly. "We've a wall of honor for those *Tupay* who have given the ultimate sacrifice of their soul for our way of life."

"But, what would happen if the *Tupay* was trapped and made a decision to turn and become a *Taqe?*"

Victor's eyes narrowed upon the trainee. "He would be the ultimate traitor to his own kind! That would be like you turning from your own country as a patriot and deciding to side with the enemy who killed you as you climbed that cliff on D-Day."

Jeff was horrified by that thought. "That would never happen. I'm faithful to my country, to the people I was sent to protect. I am faithful to you, my lord and to the *Tupay* way."

Victor gave the trainee a wide smile. "That's right, my boy. If you were ever to be caught in the net of loving energy, then all you have to remember is that you're siding with the enemy. Your patriotism to the *Tupay* would be tested but I know you'd pass that test. I can see the look in your eyes." Victor chuckled, very pleased.

"Look," Lothar said urgently, "they're moving!"

Turning, Victor saw the woman *Taqe* leaving the bank of the lake for the teahouse. "Come on, we're going to hide in this forest and let them pass by. Keep your shields up. I don't want Black to detect us."

"And then what?" Lothar asked, climbing off the trail and following his leader.

"We wait and watch. Black had the topo map open. Chances are, they are going to another lake. We'll just be patient, bide our time and see what their choice is." He laughed and moved more deeply into the shadowy forest, feeling a sense of triumph.

Chapter 12

"Time for a break," Colt told Shelly as they walked into the hotel. It was nearly 4:00 p.m. by the time they were finished hiking and had gotten back to the hotel. He managed a slight smile. "Apple pie and ice cream?" He wanted to erase that worry in her expression.

Shelly laughed and suddenly felt giddy. She welcomed anything positive to strike a balance against the attack that occurred hours earlier. Her heart felt wide-open toward Colt. His eyes danced with happiness as he guided her into the Portobello Market and Fresh Bakery. The outdoor patio sported redwood siding with iron chairs and round tables

covered with white linen. "Why not? Life's short."
Shelly knew this was the only restaurant open at this
hour. A waiter took them to a table at one end of the
sidewalk. Parallel to the outdoor dining area was a
large garden bed filled with fragrant pink roses. To
Shelly's delight, they were placed next to the gorgeous plants. The menu was deli style and casual.
There were selections of freshly baked doughnuts,
pastries, soups, sandwiches, pastas and pizzas.

The patio portion of the restaurant wasn't very
busy at this time of day. Inside, there were plenty of
comfortable couches along with a specialty coffee
bar. Today, she'd rather be outside in the fresh
mountain air. Shelly ordered a mocha latte and Colt
had dessert along with a cup of rich Colombian
coffee. Shelly sat opposite him at the table. "Do you
think we should go to Moraine Lake tomorrow
morning? It's sort of late to try it today."

Nodding, Colt pulled the map out of his pack
and opened it. "I'm exhausted from the attack, along
with that hike. I want a night to sleep and recharge.
We're going to have to be alert for our hike at
Moraine Lake." He opened the topo and eased it
over to where Shelly sat. "We can drive right up to
the lodge. It sits on the shore of the lake."

Shelly studied the map. "Sounds like a plan to
me. These lakes are so quiet and smooth that it's
easy to canoe around on them."

"We should pack a lunch and dinner for tomorrow. No telling how long this will take." Colt had
to continue to ignore how Shelly affected him emo-
tionally and physically. She looked exhausted. The
attack had taken a lot out of both of them. He
realized it but he didn't think she did.

The waitress brought their coffee and Colt's pie.
He quickly folded up the map and put it away. Shelly
grinned as he dug into the dessert. In many ways, he
was like a little boy. There was no effort on his part
to hide his joy over the pie. Shelly appreciated that
he showed her the real man beneath the protective
walls.

"It's great to see you enjoying that apple pie," she
teased, sipping her mocha latte. If she ate dessert
now, it would ruin her dinner. They had a reservation for 6:00 p.m. at the restaurant.

Wiping his mouth with a white linen napkin, Colt
said, "We didn't get many sweets as kids. That was
probably good. I'm not overweight and I ate good
food off the land instead." He patted his flat
stomach. "Now, I can pick and choose."

Shelly nodded. Looking around, she saw two
men saunter down the sidewalk to the open-air café.
Immediately, her warning bells went off, and her
heart raced for no reason. As she watched them, her
skin started to crawl. "Colt? See those two men?
They're twins. I'm getting a danger signal from

them. What do you pick up?" She opened herself up to see their auras. They sat down at the opposite end of the café. Moving her gaze back to him, she added, "I see some dirty colors in their astral fields. What do you feel?"

Having finished dessert, Colt looked across the wide room. The male twins were studying their menus before a waitress took their order. As tired as he was, Colt forced himself to move into his altered state so he could see through his third eye. "Yes, I see what you mean," he said. Why hadn't he picked up on them? Colt knew why: it was the residual loss of energy after the attack by the Skin Walker. Right now, he was vulnerable—and so was Shelly.

"Are you feeling as threatened as I am?" she asked in a low tone.

"Yes," he said, unhappy. "Do you notice that their auras are very similar to Trip Nelson's aura, the one I think is the sorcerer in your dream?"

Her eyes went wide and she whispered, "Are there three new sorcerers after us?"

With a grimace, Colt muttered, "Very possible." Three, not one. Instantly, Colt drew upon his last reserves and placed a bubble of protection around them. He'd pay for it tonight, but right now he was feeling frantic over this new bombshell. Three!

Shelly saw Colt pick up his pack and stand. She did the same. Walking to the door which would lead them into the lobby, Shelly shivered. The twins, both young men with red hair and green eyes, followed them with their gaze as they left the patio. Shelly was glad Colt didn't walk by them. As if nothing menacing was happening, the atmosphere in the restaurant was inviting and people sat on the couches enjoying their coffee.

Once inside the lobby, Shelly stuck close to Colt. Just being near him made her feel a lot more secure than the situation warranted. She glanced up at the round chandelier that hung over the area. They moved through the busy lobby.

Shelly stole a quick look around. The twins had not followed them. *Good.*

Colt slipped his hand around her elbow and guided her toward the bank of elevators. He was alert. The hair on the back of his neck still stood up, and his heart slammed into his chest. There, sitting in the lobby, was Trip Nelson. He watched them like a coyote watching a herd of sheep. Stomach knotted, adrenaline suddenly pouring into his bloodstream, Colt reinforced the protection around them. The look in Nelson's eyes was flat and dead. It sent a powerful chill up his spine.

Mouth tightening, Colt placed Shelly on the other side of him.

"What?"

"Nelson's here, too," he warned her in a hushed

tone. They slipped around the corner. An elevator was open and he guided Shelly into it.

"All three of them are here?" Shelly's voice rose in fear. Suddenly, she felt chilled to the bone. Mouth dry, a lump forming in her throat, Shelly wanted to scream. She wanted to run away from the evil that multiplied around them.

The doors shut and they moved to their floor. Colt kept his hand around her elbow and she had pressed up against him. He felt her terror. "I'd bet everything that Nelson is possessed by the sorcerer in your dream. And the twins are possessed by some of his assistants. Sorcerers can and do work together with one another when there's reason to."

"Oh, no…" Shelly uttered, her knees feeling wobbly. All she wanted to do right now was run away. "Why are they all here, Colt? This is crazy!"

The doors opened. Colt led her down the thickly carpeted hall to the door of his room. He slid the card in and opened the door. "Come on in for a while," he told her. Right now, Shelly was shaken to her core. Her idealist's world filled with good had just been shattered. Colt needed to try to figure out what was going on.

After shutting the door, Colt placed his pack in the closet and sat down on an overstuffed couch. He replaced his hiking boots with a pair of running shoes. "Have a seat," he invited.

Shelly's eyes were round with fright, and she glanced at the door. "Do you think they'll try to come up here after us?"

"I doubt it. Remember, Shelly, they want something from us. I've been trying to figure it all out. Otherwise, why would they have waited this long to hit us? Somehow, they know about the emerald sphere. Did they intercept our dreams? Maybe Yellow Teeth intercepted mine because a Skin Walker can do that. And that's the assumption I'm going on. That emerald is a lot more important than we realize. But do they know what the value of it is? That's the only logic I can find to explain why they trail but don't attack us."

Sitting down next to him on the couch, arms wrapped around her torso, Shelly muttered, "I've been beating my head for answers on this, too. I think you're right, Colt." She tucked her lower lip between her teeth and tried to fight her trepidation. She would be no help to Colt in an attack if she was not focused.

Finishing the knot on his second running shoe, Colt saw how upset Shelly had become. He broke his own rule and slid his arm around her shoulders and said, "Come here…"

Shelly sighed as Colt brought her into his arms. She rested her cheek against his shoulder and eased her arm around his narrow waist. "I'm shook up because we have three sorcerers stalking us," she whispered unsteadily. "Actually four of them. Yellow Teeth is part of this. I'm not used to cat-and-mouse games with sorcerers. I'm sorry I'm so shaken up, Colt. You were right—not knowing about evil and how to deal with it does put me at a disadvantage."

She fitted beautifully against him. Colt closed his eyes and hungrily absorbed her softness and curves. Her hair tickled his chin and he inhaled her spicy sweetness. When her arm wound across his waist, a yearning grew deep within Colt's lower body. "Right now we need to stay alert," he told her, his voice rough and oddly off-key. "We can't afford to be thinking about anything else." He said the words but didn't want to mean them.

Shelly rested her cheek against his chest, felt the stretch of fabric beneath. Leaning against Colt seemed like the most right thing in the world. She heard the slow thud of his heart and felt the monitored strength of his arms around her. "I guess I'm afraid to die," she admitted, closing her eyes, "It's one thing to have a dream warn me about a deadly sorcerer. And quite another to see the threat come to life."

"Right," Colt breathed. Oh, how he wanted to kiss Shelly! And yet, he knew it would be the stupidest thing in the world to do right now. It entered his mind that these other sorcerers might try to kidnap them. Or one of them. Was he picking up telepathically on their thoughts? But why would they do such a thing? Colt had never heard of a sorcerer ever kidnapping anyone. He sat there with the woman he'd come to love. Under any other circumstances, he'd lean down and press small, light kisses across her hair, her soft, fragrant skin and find those lips that reminded him of a flower in bloom. But not now.

"What do you think we should do?" she asked in a quiet voice. Sensing that Colt was distracted, Shelly waited.

"I don't know—yet." Colt didn't want to lie to Shelly, but he also didn't want to further alarm her if his imagination was making up a kidnapping plot. Sometimes it was hard to tell what was real telepathy versus his own imagination. Colt wasn't very good at telepathy, although he could do it from time to time. Shelly wasn't a telepath, so she couldn't confirm or deny what he had picked up on. Frustrated, Colt lifted his hand and smoothed several strands of her copper hair. "We know these three have the same signature in their aura."

"So the twins might be possessed by other sorcerers who are working with the sorcerer in Trip Nelson's body?"

"More than likely, that would be my best guess," Colt muttered, brows drawing downward. "Nelson feels like the one in charge to me."

Shelly snuggled more deeply into his arms. "I'm so glad you're here, Colt. You have really good powers of observation and training. I hunt for vortexes, that's all." Just feeling his arms contract for a moment and give her an embrace made some of her fear disperse. As much as Shelly wanted to sit up, frame Colt's face and kiss him until they melted hotly into one another, she knew it wouldn't be a good move. Her lower body ached for him and his exploring touch. No man had ever made her feel this way. The keening deep in her body was a newfound hunger she'd never known existed until now. What would it be like to love Colt completely? Blinking, Shelly grimly resolved to put her selfish desires aside. They were being stalked now. Their lives were at stake and she knew it.

"I think we need to change the game," Colt said. When she looked up at him, her lips so close to his, he inwardly groaned. "We need to get out of here. There is a lodge over at Moraine Lake. It's a good place to go since it will be our next place to search for those boulders and vortex."

Sitting up, Shelly said, "That's a great idea." Giving him an admiring look, she lifted her hand and grazed his cheek. She could feel the stubble beneath her fingertips and it excited her. "My cell phone is in my day pack."

"Get it," he said. "I'll cancel our reservation here

after we get over to the new lodge. We'll pack up and go down the exit stairs. That way, no one at the front desk will know we're gone and the rooms will still be in our names. We'll go to the parking lot, get our car and take off. Call over to the Moraine Lake Lodge and get rooms for us, make up some different names for us so we can't be tracked that way. And pay for the rooms in cash. That way, your credit card can't be found."

Nodding, Shelly got up and went to her pack. "Will they know we're going?"

He shook his head. "No, it's impossible. I have us completely shielded in a bubble of protection. They can't pick up on us in any way, shape or form."

"Good." She grabbed the cell phone and walked into the bedroom to make the call. Just having an escape plan abated some of her fear.

Colt started packing his suitcase. Moments later, Shelly emerged from his bedroom. "Did you get the new reservation?" he asked.

"Yes. I reserved a room for us."

Colt felt a ribbon of triumph because they were going to leave the sorcerers behind. "I'll keep up the protection so they'll think we're still here." Never mind how the exhaustion was eating at the corners of his energy. Right now, Colt knew his will was making the difference. He was damned if a group of sorcerers would take them down.

Putting the cell phone away, Shelly sighed with relief. "I lied and changed our names. We're now Susan and Paul Hornsby."

"Good. That way the sorcerers won't find us by our real names." He kept mum about the fact that some highly skilled sorcerers could pick up a person's energy trail and follow it. Time would tell how skilled these sorcerers were. He would wipe out their trail energetically to ensure they couldn't follow them. Grimly, he added, "Tomorrow morning we'll start off at dawn and slip down to the canoe rental and be off before we can be identified by anyone."

"Do you think they know where we'll be searching next?"

"I don't know. They've been able to follow us easily because we're here under our real names and with my passport. That's going to change now."

"I'm glad," Shelly said, relief in her voice as she hoisted the pack onto her right shoulder.

"Sorcerers vary in their experience and abilities," Colt told her, walking her to the door. He was going to escort her down to her room and help her pack. At this point, he didn't want Shelly out of his sight. "We don't know the extent of their skills." He opened the door a crack and then peeked out. The hall was empty. Taking her hand, Colt led her out into the hall and swiftly walked down to her room.

Shelly quickly packed, Colt hoisted the black piece of luggage to his room and she followed with her day pack on her back. There was a sense of urgency. She shut the door and followed Colt into his bedroom. "I'm feeling really unsettled, Colt. It's as if they're waiting for us or are going to spring a trap on us."

"I know," he said, making sure he had left nothing in the room that could be a clue. "The sooner we get out of here, the better."

"Now!" VICTOR GROWLED at his men. The three of them dashed out of the elevator to the floor where they knew the *Taqe* were staying. No one was in the hall as they moved swiftly toward the first door. Victor had gotten cards for both rooms by hypnotizing a clerk and making her create them.

After sliding the card into Shelly's room door, Victor burst in. The twins would hit Colt's room down the hall. Once inside, he halted. It was empty! Moving quickly, Victor scanned the bedroom. Nothing! He quickly checked every corner, including the bathroom. The female *Taqe*'s energy was not present! Breathing hard, Victor went to the closet and slid it open. There were no clothes. Turning, he moved over to the dresser. He opened all of the drawers—also empty.

"What is going on here?" he snarled. Turning on

his heel, he raced out of the room. As he jerked open the door and stepped out into the hall, he saw Lothar and Jeff standing outside Colt's room. The look on their faces was one of surprise. Hurrying down the hall, he asked, "Why are you out here?"

Lothar said, "My lord, he's gone. We checked everywhere. No sign of luggage, clothes or him."

"Same here," Victor said, unhappy. Looking up and down the hall, he kept his voice low. "They must have known of our plan. Somehow they picked up on it!"

"Kidnapping the girl was a good idea," Lothar said. "We were shielded. How could they have picked up on our thoughts?"

Rubbing his chin, Victor said, "I have no idea. But they know who we are now. I saw that earlier. The auras on these three we've possessed look the same. Black must have put it together. He realizes we're sorcerers and have possessed these three bodies."

"They're smarter than I thought," Jeff murmured. "Because I know I've shielded my thoughts from them. And neither of them are telepaths according to their aura signatures."

Hands on his hips, Victor felt rage. "Who could have tipped them off, then? Is there a third person to their party who is a telepath?"

Groaning, Lothar said, "My lord, we always

assumed they'd only put out two people on a mission."

"I know, I know!" Victor paced the hall, the anger consuming him. "They've outwitted us." Victor refused to give voice to an even worse thought: that the male Warrior for the Light had extraordinary telepathic abilities, good enough to pick up on what they were planning even though they were fully shielded. That was not a good sign. Black was far more dangerous than Victor wanted to admit.

Jeff traded looks with Lothar. He was about to speak, but Lothar gave him a warning shake of his head. Being a knight, Lothar knew Guerra much better than Jeff did. He remained silent as the Dark Lord paced angrily up and down in front of them.

Finally, as Victor slowed his pacing, Lothar spoke. "My lord, they are gone. I was thinking about where they might be now."

Jerking his head up, Victor glared at Lothar. "Pray tell, where do you think they've gone?"

"I was talking to the waiter earlier, after the *Taqe* left the restaurant. He overheard them talking about Moraine Lake."

Raising his brows, Victor felt a surge of hope. "You're sure?"

Lothar beamed. "Yes, my lord."

Victor patted him heartily on the shoulders. "Good man!"

Feeling the Dark Lord's joy, Lothar leaked a slight smile. "I always want to please you."

Jeff whistled softly. "So they might be at the lodge over at Moraine Lake?"

"Maybe," Victor said. "I've already sent out a feeler to find them, but it was rebuffed and came back to me. Black is protecting them fully and we can't get inside that protective wall he's thrown up. No, we're going to have to drive over there and see if we can spot them. From our research, we know the woman drives a blue Honda. We know what kind of car Black rented. Let's look for them in the parking lot first. If we find them, we know they're at the lodge. Then, all we have to do is wait them out."

Rubbing his hands together, his eyes gleaming with pleasure, Victor said, "First, let's dump these bodies and get three new ones. They know what we look like now."

"But, my lord, won't we have the same aura as these three did?" Jeff asked.

"No. Not always," Victor said grumpily. "Oh, I'm sure Black will figure it out eventually, but he's human. He won't see the twins and Nelson. Even though he might see our auras initially, he won't put it together, and that may give us just enough time to nail them."

Chapter 13

Shelly felt relief as they got their new room at the Moraine Lake Lodge. This time, they were Mr. and Mrs. Paul Hornsby. She closed the door and watched as Colt carried their luggage into the bedroom. They were posing as a married couple so no more separate rooms. Shelly wanted this arrangement. In another way, they didn't need such an obvious distraction. But what else could they do under the circumstances?

The appointments in the room were gorgeous and as she stood in front of a picture window that overlooked the deeply turquoise Moraine Lake, she appreciated its natural beauty. The groups of lodges sat up on a hill above the lake. The evening was upon them, the sun having slipped down below the Rocky Mountains, the shadows deep across the calm lake. She saw a canoe coming in, the colors bright against the blue of the glacially fed waters.

Frowning, Shelly moved from the suite's window overlooking the lake and walked into their bedroom. She watched as Colt hung clothes in the closet. There was tension in his profile. She went over and pulled open one of the drawers to the dresser.

"Do you still feel it?"

"Yes," he said, turning and looking over at her. Her brow was wrinkled and there was somberness in her hazel gaze. "I feel like we were just attacked back there at the other hotel."

"Me, too," Shelly said softly. "I felt the attack." She rubbed her arms and frowned. "It looks like my psychic awareness is opening up to include evil." Putting her clothes away in the drawers, she added, "This isn't a game."

Colt went over, drew her into his arms and embraced her. "Right now, we're ahead of them. We've changed hotels and names. They can't find us unless they see us and we're going to do everything we can to minimize that factor." Silently, Colt prayed that his massive wall prevented them from finding them telepathically. But for how long would it hold? He was beyond exhaustion at this point.

Shelly slid her arms around his muscular frame and pressed her head against his shoulder. "I knew this was serious business, but now it's really coming to rest on me. They want to kill us."

"I know," he murmured. After pressing a quick, chaste kiss to her hair, Colt eased Shelly away from him. If he didn't, he would push the luggage off the bed and lay her down beside him. The desire to make love to her was more than an ache now. Hands on her shoulders, he looked down into her worried eyes. "We'll be okay. We'll order room service. If they're nosing around trying to find us, we aren't available to be seen. As soon as I'm done unpacking, I'll call the desk and get that canoe rental for an hour before sunrise. It will be pretty dark then and tough to make us out if they happen to be snooping around."

"All sensible strategies," she said. Right now, Colt seemed calm and unaffected by the danger. But she knew better. He was just as threatened by it as she was, yet his calm demeanor soothed her. Reaching up, she touched his cheek. "You're a very brave person."

"Me?" Colt gave her a derisive look. His cheek tingled pleasantly beneath the grazing touch of her fingers. A fierce need rose in him.

"Courage is what we need, isn't it? Maybe there is a symbolic purpose to our hunt for this sphere. About facing our fears and walking through them in order to find it."

"Yes to all of those questions," Colt muttered. "Neither of us realized at the beginning what we were walking into."

"I wonder if we had, if we'd have pursued this emerald?" Shelly wondered. She eased out of his arms because all she wanted to do was kiss Colt senseless. Instead, she sat down on the bed, hands folded into her lap. She gave him a wry look. "I was never afraid until now. Oh, I've heard lots of stories about sorcerers over the years, but I've never had any experience with them." Shrugging, she added, "I guess until you have a confrontation with a sorcerer, you don't get it."

Opening a drawer of the dresser, Colt began to put his clothes away. His hands literally itched to keep Shelly in his embrace. If he was busy with clothes, he wouldn't do it. "Innocence is a good thing up to a point," he told her.

"In this case, ignorance is not bliss." Worriedly, Shelly looked toward the open door that led into the living room. "I keep feeling in my gut that this sorcerer and his men are onto us. I ask myself, what would I do if I were in his shoes? What if he's invaded our rooms and hasn't found us there? What would he do next?"

"If I were him, I'd start a search for the car I rented. And putting your Honda at another nearby hotel will throw them off our track." Colt didn't know the abilities of these men. That made this situation even more dangerous.

"And how smart of you to change our rental car at the Samson Mall in Lake Louise before we came to this lodge."

"Right. I try to think like them the best I can," Colt said, pushing the drawer closed and opening the one below it. "If I were him I would try to track us by the car. The fact we turned it in at the mall and rented another one from another company is going to throw them off our trail." *For a while,* but he didn't add that.

"I wouldn't know if they were trying to read my mind," Shelly said, unhappy with her lack of certain paranormal skills.

"I would. And that hasn't happened because I have strong energy walls in place to protect us. And if they can't read our thoughts and follow that energy trail to where we are now, they're blind."

"I hope so," Shelly said fervently. "I live in abject fear of being possessed." Shivering, she added, "I just don't want either of us ending up like that."

Colt zipped his luggage shut and placed it in the closet. He came over and sat at her side. "We didn't know how dangerous this game was going to be. Stop blaming yourself."

Shelly grimaced and nodded.

"I know they want something from us," Colt said. "They'd rather have us alive so it has to be about this emerald sphere we're trying to find. I'd sure like to know more about this emerald." He looked around the quiet room. "I'm going to sleep out there on the couch. You get the bedroom."

Glumly, Shelly agreed. "It's not what I want, but you're right."

"I know," Colt whispered. He reached out and touched her hair. It was incredibly silky and soft beneath his exploring fingertips. "Also, did you see there's no way to escape from this suite if they break in here? They'll have us trapped. I wish we could have gotten a ground-floor room because they have doors that lead outside. That would have been good to escape but we don't have the option."

"I feel the sorcerer is hunting us right now. My gut tells me that."

"Yes," Colt confirmed, studying the hotel door. "We're going to have to stay on the move. We can't trust that we'll be safe here more than a day. I'm already thinking that after we search Moraine Lake's shores we need to move again. It's the only way to stay ahead of them, Shelly."

VICTOR CURSED SOFTLY beneath his breath. He and his two men had gathered in the lobby of the hotel at Lake Louise. They sat huddled on three over-stuffed chairs as the flow of traffic continued around them. It was dinnertime and many of the patrons were coming in from their day's adventures to get changed and eat.

"Well?" Victor snapped. "What next? What would you do if you were them? We've scoured the whole parking-lot area from one end to another. The woman's car is gone. The Toyota rented by Black is gone."

Jeff looked over at the check-in area of the massive hotel. There were three car-company booths for the three largest car-rental companies. "Is it possible Black turned in his Prius and then rented another type of car? Or they used the woman's car? That would explain why we didn't find it."

"I can go over and pick the minds of those three people manning the rental booths," Lothar suggested.

Victor knew that if they did a mind probe on those young people, it would leave them in shock and unable to talk coherently for an hour or more. He couldn't risk doing it right now with the hotel filled with patrons. Someone would notice. "Not now. Too many onlookers around. We don't want to draw attention to ourselves at all."

"Well," Lothar said, trying to cheer up Victor, "I like my new body."

Grimacing, Victor said nothing. They'd gone into the woods on a trail far from the hotel. There, they'd found three male family members and taken possession of them. Victor had taken the father, Lothar possessed the uncle and Jeff took the seventeen-year-old boy's body. The other three bodies were dragged off the trail and hidden so that hungry grizzly bears would find them before anyone else did. The danger in taking a body was that someone from this hotel would miss them. Trip Nelson worked as a guide. When he didn't show up, there would be concern. And Victor knew that the employer would start looking for him in earnest within hours of his disappearance.

Lothar was now a thirty-eight-year-old blond Canadian from Toronto named Charles Hampton. The man worked for a publisher in that city. His brother, Harvey, was forty, in tip-top athletic shape and worked as the vice president of a transport company in the same city. The son, Brian Hampton, was terribly good-looking and very athletic. Victor had wanted someone young and strong in case they needed to chase down the *Taqe*.

"A missing rental car," Victor pondered. He glanced toward the clerks at the auto booths. "We really do need to read their minds. Let's wait until later. After dinner. By 11:00 p.m., things will quiet down in the lobby."

Nodding, Lothar said, "Let me do it."

"Sounds like a good strategy," Victor said.

Jeff picked up on the thoughts of the Dark Lord. Inwardly, he reeled from the quickness of all that had happened to him. Even more, he felt badly for possessing these innocent people. Jeff had not realized how often it was done. His family values made him uncomfortable with this, but he didn't dare voice that. "Is there another way to get that information on their rental car?"

"What?" Victor snapped beneath his breath. "Go over and ask them?"

Jeff shrugged. "Why not? I could do that. If I can find out something, isn't it worth the try?" He suddenly found himself wanting to protect these humans. Why? Having no answer, he waited for the Dark Lord.

Lothar rolled his eyes. "He's a young *Tupay,*" was all he said.

"Go ahead," Victor invited silkily. The stupid trainee would find out the hard way that mind probes were a very quick, efficient way to get information. He'd get nothing from these clerks right now.

Rising, Jeff knew that neither older spirit believed he could get any information. In a pair of long canvas shorts, a red T-shirt and hiking boots, Jeff was sure he presented the picture of a typical teenager to everyone. The fact that the clerks were all in their early twenties at the booths could make for a bonding of sorts. "I'll give it a try," he told them. Inwardly, he wanted to save these three young men from the pain and agony of a mind probe if he could.

As he walked over to the first rental booth, Jeff knew that his morals and values were not entirely the same as those of his fellow *Tupay*. Perhaps, over time, he would become hardened like Victor and Lothar. For now, however, his conscience ate at him.

"Hi," he greeted the black-haired young clerk, "I'm looking for some friends of mine. I just arrived here and I was supposed to meet Mr. Black here in the lobby."

"Yes, I have him listed here." The clerk frowned and studied his computer. "But I have him checking out earlier today."

"Oh?" Jeff tried to modulate his voice so that it showed surprise and confusion. "Are you sure?"

"Yes," he said.

"Well…did he rent another car or did he go with the rental he had?"

The clerk studied the computer some more. "Oh, I see what happened here. Your friend turned in his car and then it was cleaned. About two hours later, another party rented it."

"Did he rent another car?" Jeff asked.

"If he did, it wasn't from us." The clerk turned to

the competing rental booth and asked the clerk. Jeff waited. That clerk checked his computer.

"No, sorry. No such name here. Let me ask Tolly over here…"

Jeff got a shake of the clerk's head from the third rental booth.

"Nope, I don't recognize his name," one clerk said apologetically.

"Mr. Black asked if there was another car rental here at Lake Louise. I told him there was one at Samson Mall, about two miles down the road from this hotel."

Going back to Victor, Jeff told him he was going to drive over to the mall and check it out. Victor agreed.

Jeff went into the mall. He stepped over to the red-haired clerk. "I'm looking for Colt Black," he pressed. "My dad was supposed to meet him here, but maybe they got the wrong car rental. Can you check your rentals from early this morning?"

"Sure," the clerk said enthusiastically. Typing into his computer, he said, "There was one car rental to a Mr. and Mrs. Paul and Susan Hornsby. There is no Colt Black listed."

"Okay," Jeff said, leaning over the desk. "What kind of car did they rent?"

"A 2010 red Toyota Prius."

"Great. Where did they say they were going?"

"According to the computer, they were renting it for a week but there was no destination other than bringing it back here to us."

Frowning, Jeff said, "Hey, that's okay. Thanks, I'll let my dad know. Maybe they're at another hotel near here."

"Well, let me help you," the clerk said with a smile. He tore off a piece of paper. "This is a list of all the hotels in the park. What you might do is call around and see if you can locate them."

Taking the paper with the hotel names, addresses and phone numbers, Jeff grinned. "Thanks, dude. You've been a big help. I think my dad and uncle just got the wrong hotel."

Triumphant, Jeff tried to keep the glee out of his voice. He walked over and handed the paper to Victor. "My lord," he said, excitement in his tone, "I believe we have their new names and identification on their rented car. Black probably switched names. I can't be sure about this, but it might be a lead."

Chapter 14

Lothar wiped his smarting eyes before he entered the Moraine Lake Lodge. The watch on his hairy wrist read 4:00 a.m. They had spent the night driving from one lodge to another in Banff National Park, trying to locate the red Toyota Prius. They hadn't realized how many Canadians were "green" and how many had the damn hybrid automobile. The light on the eastern horizon was barely silhouetting the rugged Rockies as he hesitated at the stairs. Victor and Jeff halted.

"Okay, you know what to do," Victor said.

Nodding, Lothar said, "Of course."

"How many idiots have this stupid Prius?" Victor griped unhappily, looking around at the dark, quiet area. The lodge was lit but the lake was dark and black. An owl hooted in a nearby fir, the call making Victor feel even more frustrated. He was angered by the disappearance of the *Taqe*.

"A lot," Jeff murmured. It was cool and he had a hoodie on, hands in the pockets for warmth.

Giving Lothar a sharp gesture, Victor snarled, "Well, there are *two* red Toyota Priuses in this parking lot. Go in there and find out."

Yawning, Lothar nodded, turned and quickly took the steps. As he pushed open the door, he saw the lobby was empty. A sleepy-eyed male clerk with black hair and brown eyes sat at the desk. He perked up a bit as Lothar approached.

In his most diplomatic voice, Lothar said, "I'm so sorry to bother you, but my uncle, who was very tired, just grazed a red Toyota Prius out in your lot. We were coming over here for breakfast at 6:00 a.m." Lothar gave him a pleading look. "Can you tell me who owns the Prius? We need to leave our name, address and phone number to contact them about this little accident."

"Oh…sure," the clerk murmured. "Was it a bad accident?"

"Oh, no," Lothar said. "Just a scratch."

Going to his computer, the clerk typed in some

info. "Well, there are two red Priuses here right now."

Lothar got out his notebook and a pen from the bag he carried, and said, "I didn't get the license plate. Can you give me both names and their room numbers?"

"Uh, I'm sorry, sir, but we aren't allowed to give out room numbers."

"Oh," Lothar feigned, "that's right. Names are fine." He poised the pen on the counter.

"Mr. and Mrs. Winn Drake and Mr. and Mrs. Paul Hornsby."

Heart leaping, Lothar pretended nonchalance and dutifully wrote down the names. "Thank you so much." He turned and left.

Victor waited impatiently at the bottom of the stairs in a foul mood. The physical body needed sleep and he was grouchy. Lothar had a look of glee on his face.

"Well?" he snapped.

"They're here!" he said triumphantly, joining them.

Perking up, Victor grinned. "Good. Do you have a room number?"

"They refuse to give them out."

"No matter. Jeff, go in there and mind probe that clerk. Get the room number for the so-called Mr. and Mrs. Paul Hornsby." Was that Black and the woman?

Victor hoped so. The only way to find out was to break in and see.

"Right."

Victor looked up. The stars were close and bright. The dawn was edging the mountains. "I'd like nothing better than to catch them unawares," he told Lothar.

"Do you think capturing them is the best idea?"

"There's nothing like a threat to get one of them to spill their information to us," Victor said.

"So if it is Black and the woman, you're going to tell one of them that you'll possess the other? They know what that means."

"Yes. I have to vary my tactics and strategy every time the *Taqe* send out a team. The last mission was easy. This one hasn't been. First, we'll verify it is them. Next, we'll figure out which one knows the most. Then, we'll threaten that person so that he or she will give us what we need. After that, we'll take them to wherever it is and let them retrieve the emerald sphere."

Lothar chuckled. "That's a good plan. They won't be expecting us to have a card to get into their room. I imagine they're feeling pretty smug and safe about now."

"Asleep and unaware," Victor said, grinning in anticipation. He heard the door open and close. Jeff came down the stairs.

"Room 401."

"Good!" Victor looked around. "First, let's case this place and find out where all the exits are on that floor. I want to know they're there before we attack. This time, we're going to get them…."

COLT AWOKE WITH A JERK. Disoriented for a moment, he felt a sizzling sense of danger. Throwing off the blanket, he stood up in his boxer shorts. He twisted around and looked toward the door. The sorcerers had found them! Hissing a curse between his teeth, he ran to the bedroom. Opening the door, he called to Shelly. She was asleep, the sheet pulled up to her waist. The cotton nightgown with the pink ribbon around the oval neck did nothing but make her look incredibly beautiful.

"Shelly! Wake up!"

Instantly, she jerked awake. "What?"

"We've gotta get out of here. Now! I can feel them!"

Disoriented, Shelly threw off the sheet and leaped out of bed. "But…how?"

Grabbing a T-shirt from the drawer, Colt pulled it over his head. "I don't know. It doesn't matter. Hurry and get dressed. Take only the pack. The cell phones are in there, right?"

Sleep torn from her, Shelly lurched toward the drawers. "Uh…yes…yes…"

They quickly got into their jeans and hiking boots, grabbed their coats and hitched up their knapsacks onto their shoulders. Within five minutes, Colt was cracking the door to their room. He peered out into the hall. It was quiet. Heart pounding, he turned and whispered, "Come on. We'll take the exit stairs."

Shelly followed and they ran lightly down the carpeted hall to the exit door. Adrenaline pounded through her. Mind spinning with shock, she slipped through the door and quietly closed it behind her. Taking the flights of concrete stairs, they made it down to the first floor.

Colt hesitated inside the door. There was a rectangular glass window on it. Carefully, he looked one way and then the other. The hall seemed deserted. "Let's go," he rasped, opening the door. It squeaked. He froze.

Shelly crowded up to his side. "What?"

"The noise of the door," he said. Sweat trickled down his temple. He felt hot and nearly suffocated in the jacket. Outdoors, it was in the forties and he knew he'd need it.

"Can we get to the car?"

"That's where we're going." Again, he eased the door open a little more. It didn't squeak. "Let's go!"

They hurried down the empty hall to the rear door that led to the parking lot. The cold of the morning hit them. Shelly followed Colt closely.

Looking around, she felt terror. Every deep shadow along the lodge wall turned into a man waiting to jump them. Mouths dry, they left the safety of the building and moved into the trees that surrounded the huge parking lot.

"Damn!"

The word exploded softly from Colt. Shelly ran into him. He'd stopped so suddenly she didn't have a chance to halt. The sulfur lamps showed the parking lot clearly. As Shelly caught herself and looked where Colt was focused, she gasped. There, standing alongside their red Prius, was a man. A young man in a hoodie.

"His aura. It's the same as Nelson's. He's a sorcerer, Colt. They know our car," Shelly whispered, grabbing onto Colt's upper arm. "What are we going to do?"

As he scanned the area, Colt knew they were safe in the trees. "Let me think," he growled. He'd thrown up a powerful bubble of protection that made them invisible to anyone, even a sorcerer. Watching the man near their Prius, Colt was satisfied the protection was working because he wasn't picking up on them.

Dawn was coming, but it was still dark in the valley. "We need to get to the canoe livery. They won't expect us down there. Chances are they're in the hotel and already in our room." He glared toward the lodge.

Shelly gulped, her pulse pounding with abject fear. The young man at the Prius didn't seem to be aware of them and that was good. Her fingers dug into the down jacket Colt wore. "The canoe?"

"We have to get out of here," he rasped. "They obviously expected us to go to the car. That's why there's a guard. We have to start thinking about what they won't expect us to do."

"When they find us gone, though, they'll come out here looking for us."

"I'm guessing they will," Colt said harshly. He turned and gently gripped Shelly's arm. "We have money, food in our knapsacks, bottles of water and cell phones—everything we need to keep on point to locate this emerald. That sphere is a lot more important than we realized from our dreams. We wouldn't have so many sorcerers after us if it weren't." He shook his head and added, "We'll use the trees as cover. They go right down to the canoe livery." Colt searched her fearful expression. He wanted to say everything was going to be all right, but he didn't know if it would be. Yellow Teeth was somewhere. Colt wasn't picking up on him but he knew the Skin Walker wasn't far away. Heart pounding in his chest, he felt an overwhelming need to protect Shelly against all of them. She was just as necessary on this hunt for the sphere as he was. Each had skills that would help to find the emerald. He gave her a tight smile. "Ready to follow me?"

Nodding, Shelly gulped, "Yes, let's go. If we can get a canoe and paddle away and hide in the darkness of the lake along the shore, they won't pick up our trail."

"That's what I'm hoping," Colt told her. He turned and started off at a slow trot within the edge of the trees. The dawn light was just enough to ensure that he wouldn't stumble and fall over limbs, exposed roots or downed branches scattered across the pine needle–strewn forest. He didn't want to move too fast for Shelly's sake. The hair on the back of his neck felt stiff and hot. Their lives were on the line. Savagely suppressing his own fear of the darkness and knowing that this was the time of day that sorcerers roamed the earth in search of a body to possess, Colt used his anger as a shield. He was damned if any sorcerer, known or unknown, was going to get to them. *No way.*

"WHERE ARE THEY?" Victor barked, looking around the empty hotel room. They had switched on the light and no one was around. Lothar came out of the bedroom looking angry.

"My lord, they somehow must have known we were coming." He triumphantly held up a billfold he'd found on the floor. Inside was a picture of Shelly Godwin. He grinned. "They were under an assumed name."

Victor jerked the blanket off the couch. He glared at the photo. "At least we know we've got the right couple. They've left their clothes here. That tells me they didn't leave very long ago."

"Jeff is at their car. He has telepathy. If he saw them, he'd call us," Lothar said, scowling as he looked around the room.

"Damn them," Victor muttered. Glaring around the room, he rubbed his chin. "They can't get to their car. So where else would they go?"

"They used a canoe at the other lakes. Why not this one?" Lothar said.

"That's it! Come on, you and I will go down to the dock. We'll leave Jeff with the car. We have to find them!"

RUNNING HARD FOR the wharf, Shelly felt her legs getting wobbly—from fear of being found by the sorcerers and not from lack of physical stamina. Colt had already arrived at the line of canoes lying up on the dock. He turned a dark green one over and slid it quietly into the water. Standing by it, he gestured for her to hurry.

The thunking of her boots sounded hollowly along the wooden wharf. Gasping, she climbed into the bow of the canoe. Colt handed her a paddle.

"Hurry!" he urged in a whisper. Leaping into the canoe at the stern, Colt pushed them off. Just about four hundred feet down from the wharf there was a thick line of trees and bushes overhanging the edge of the lake. He dug his paddle into the mirror-like water. Shelly was paddling hard. The canoe turned and they moved it as quickly as they could through the cool morning air, patches of fog hovering near the surface of the lake and into the dense brush along the shore.

Breathing hard, Colt kept looking over his shoulder. He felt the sorcerers. They were close! Would they spot them? Heart pounding like a freight train in his chest, his hands tightened around the paddle and the canoe surged forward.

VICTOR TORE DOWN the slope at a gallop, though the grass was slippery with dew. Searching the quiet, calm lake, he saw nothing. Lothar ran at his side. As they made it to the boat livery, Victor skidded to a halt. Breathless, he looked around, his eyes narrowing as he tried to ferret through the darkness and fog across the long lake. There were loons somewhere out in the darkness beginning to call to one another, their tune haunting.

"I don't see them," Lothar said, leaning over, hands on his knees, catching his breath. "Maybe they didn't come here."

Anger and frustration surged through Victor. "I don't know! Do you pick up an energy trail on them?" The problem with being in a human body was that Victor could not use all his array of detection skills due to the solidity of the form. Right now, he didn't want to get rid of the human body because it served him and his plan.

"No…nothing. What now?" Lothar said, his voice sounding defeated. "Black is a Warrior for the Light. He can protect them in a bubble and we won't find him. I'll bet that's what has happened."

Looking at his watch, Victor said, "We'll wait until 6:00 a.m. By that time, that mindless clerk we probed at the desk will be switched off with a new clerk for the day. We'll wait until then. We'll ask about the canoe rental. Someone has to show up down here and have a list of names on it."

"But if they took one now, how will the employee know?"

Sometimes, Victor wanted to scream. "Stupid, one of the canoes will be missing! That's how he'll know."

"Oh…"

Shaking his head, Victor said, "Let's go. I want to tell Jeff what has happened and what we're going to do." He could use telepathy but Victor's powers were not as strong or solid as they were in spirit. Walking along the wharf, Victor counted the canoes. There were nineteen of them. Was one missing? Had the *Taqe* taken one? Were they hidden somewhere along the edge of the lake? Until he knew,

Victor wasn't sure what to do next. If the *Taqe* had indeed stolen a canoe, then the three *Tupay* were going to check out the shore of this lake.

Lothar, sensing his concern, said as he huffed up the slope, "What if they aren't here?"

"Then we need to keep Jeff at their Prius, get in our car and drive around and look for them. There are other lodges nearby. They might have hitched a ride with someone out on the main highway. We need to drive along it and look for them."

Shaking his head, Lothar followed him down the length of the lodge toward the parking lot. "This team is slippery. Not like the other one."

Snorting, Victor growled, "The *Taqe* learned their lesson well. They're not about to send out anyone from now on that isn't smart and alert. They lost one of their team members and they're trying to stop it from happening again."

Glum, Lothar walked quickly at Victor's side once they rounded the corner of the lodge. In the distance, he saw Jeff leaning against the Prius, arms against his chest, looking bored. The dawn light was sufficient now for them to be able to read his expression. "Well," the knight griped, "if that's the case, it's harder on us, too."

"They're evolving their strategies," Victor said. "That's no surprise. They're choosing people who can run the game as quickly as we can create it."

"I just want to know how they knew we were coming."

Shrugging, Victor said, "It doesn't matter. What matters now is to find them. They're either somewhere on that lake or hitching a ride on the highway."

"YOU OKAY?" Colt asked. He dropped the canoe into the brush along the bank of the lake. Dawn was coming, a pinkish cast behind the Rockies silhouetting their jagged, snow-covered peaks. Shelly had knelt on the pine needles and was opening her pack.

"Yes, just shaky with adrenaline is all," she said.

Colt knelt opposite her and shrugged out of his own day pack. They were hidden in a grove deep within the woods. The thick wall of brush along the lakeshore was a perfect screen to hide them. His hands were scratched where he'd hauled the canoe through the bushes. "I feel the sorcerers leaving," he said. Unzipping his pack, he drew out a bottle of water and a protein bar.

Nodding, Shelly said, "Yes, they're not so close now. Even I can feel their energy isn't as strong as before." Relief made her hands less shaky.

Looking toward the lake, the predawn pink mirrored on the surface, Colt thought how beautiful and serene the lake was right now. "I feel them continuing to hunt for us. They're going in a different direction, away from us. That's good."

Taking a swig of water, Shelly asked, "What do you think they'll do next?"

Colt peeled off the wrapper of his protein bar. "I think they will figure out we've either gone to the highway to escape them because we can't get to our car or we're out here at the lake."

Brow wrinkling, Shelly said, "How could he know we're still here?"

"Sorcerers aren't stupid," Colt murmured between bites. "We took a canoe from the livery. I'm sure someone from the lodge comes on duty at six or seven o'clock. They'll count the canoes and find one missing. All they have to do is go down and ask the guy about it and that will confirm we took one."

"The sorcerers can't be sure we took it," Shelly said, feeling fear snake through her again. Colt appeared calm and self-assured. She felt like spaghetti that had been overcooked.

"Oh, I think they can," Colt said. "We can't assume they won't know, Shelly. That would put us in more danger than we're already in."

"I guess you're right," she grudgingly admitted. "Right now, I'm so scared I can hardly walk, Colt."

With a tender gaze, Colt reached out and cupped her fiery cheek. "Take some deep breaths. That's what I'd do when I was a kid and scared of the Skin Walkers walking around our hogan at night looking for a way in. It helps calm you."

The warmth of his calloused hand eased some of her fear. She touched it. "Thanks." She laughed a little, her voice high and off-pitch.

While he didn't want to remove his hand, Colt forced himself to. They kept their voices to a bare whisper even though they were surrounded by a good twenty feet of bushes on all sides. "People who work the mystical realms of life learn about the light and the dark. You've lived in the light world, but now you're learning about the dark side of it," he said, finishing off his bar. There would be no bacon and eggs today.

"I know, but the dark side always sounded so detached to me because I had never interfaced with evil before this," Shelly admitted, opening up a protein bar.

Colt gazed at the calm lake. The sun was going to rise in about an hour, around 6:00 a.m. "We have about an hour before sunrise. After we get done eating, we're going to have to start looking along the shore of the lake. The sorcerers won't be able to confirm we're here for that hour, so it gives us a head start of sorts."

"Okay, I'm ready."

After he got up and shrugged into his knapsack, Colt picked up the canoe. He turned it over so that he could hold it across his shoulders and stabilize the sides with his hands. Luckily, it was a small aluminum canoe. Moving slowly through the brush, he reached the lakeshore where there were no rocks, only soil, grass and some wildflowers along the edge where the fir and spruce trees stood. As gently as possible, Colt set the canoe down, turned it over and slid it quietly back into the water.

Shelly then climbed into the bow and picked up her paddle. Colt wanted her up front, to not only look for the twin boulders, but to feel any vortex energy that might be nearby. Quietly dipping the paddle into the water, Colt guided the canoe about three feet off the lakeshore. Ahead was a wide talus slope, and he hoped against hope that it might have the boulders they were looking for.

The water dripped and fell off the paddle with each rise and fall of his arms. The canoe was stable and Colt watched Shelly, who peered over the left side, looking for clues among the rocks. His heart wrenched within his chest. The sorcerers were still close. Colt could feel them sending out weak energetic feelers trying to locate them. Luckily for them, they were cloaked and there was no way the evil trio could find them. *One hour.* That was all they had. More than ever, Colt wanted to live to love Shelly. Would the Great Spirit give him that chance?

Chapter 15

Victor didn't wait long after giving Jeff orders to climb into their rental car and begin scouring the highway on either side of the lodge. If the two *Taqe* had escaped to the highway, Jeff would find them. On a hunch, Victor went back to the canoe wharf where Lothar was waiting for him.

"Ready?" Victor said. Lothar had taken a red canoe from the shore and slipped it in the water.

"Yes, my lord. This is a good plan. Why wait for someone to come and count canoes? If they've stolen one, we will, too. And perhaps we can find them before the day's activities begin around here."

Victor climbed in and took the bow position. "That's right. I'm assuming they did take the canoe and they're out here somewhere on this lake." Victor peered through the gloom and spotty fog as Lothar sat in the stern of the canoe and began to paddle across the placid, glass-like water. He cursed the Warrior for the Light. Black's power was much more than he'd ever anticipated, especially since he had enclosed himself and the woman in a bubble of invisibility. Narrowing his eyes, Victor began to hunt for evidence of the *Taqe* on the lake. Dawn was coming but far too slowly for his thinning patience. Much of the lake remained dark and plunged in deep shadows. He couldn't make out anything on the water. But then, Victor told himself, if he were the *Taqe,* he would hug the shoreline in hopes of not being spotted. That would be a far better strategy.

"We should know fairly soon if they're here," Lothar said, paddling strongly in the stern.

The canoe glided out of the wharf area. Moraine Lake was a north-to-south oblong lake. There were a lot more forest trees around this one and fewer talus slopes than there were around Lake Agnes, making it harder to spot the *Taqe* now. But in another hour, the light would help them to see anything on or near the shore of this glacial lake.

"See them?" Lothar asked, hope in his tone.

"No," Victor growled. "It's too dark yet." When he possessed a human, Victor lost much of his vaunted paranormal skills. Even now, looking through the eyes of his host, Victor would be hard-pressed to pick up auras. And energy trails were out of the question. "Paddle along the shore. About six feet away from it. My senses tell me they went south from here." No, they had to do this the old-fashioned way and Victor was comfortable with the situation. After all, he'd been able to steal one emerald this way. Why not another?

"Right," Lothar said. "If they're here, we'll find them."

SHELLY SUCKED IN a deep breath as she knelt in the brush about ten feet away from the lakeshore. "You were right," she whispered to Colt, who knelt at her side. Right out in front of them a red canoe with two men in it glided by.

Colt's eyes narrowed. Turning, he whispered into her ear, "That's them, but they've possessed different bodies. I can feel them and see the signs in their auras. Over at Lake Louise I didn't know what I was looking at, but now I do. They have nearly the same aura signature that Trip Nelson and those twins had over at Lake Louise." Three sorcerers! That blew Colt away. And then there was Yellow Teeth. Who were these sorcerers?

Shelly felt some relief as the canoe passed them. The man in the front was lean and about five foot ten inches tall. The taller, stouter man in the back was doing all the paddling.

"Those poor people…" Shelly whispered.

Mouth tightening, Colt slid his arm around her shoulders as they crouched tightly together. They'd stashed their bright-colored jackets, and their dark green and tan shirts would help them blend in to the landscape. After another five minutes, the canoe disappeared around a curve toward the southern end of Moraine Lake.

"We're okay for now," he told her in a normal voice. Straightening, he got up and retrieved their jackets. He handed Shelly hers and they put them back on because it was chilly.

"What now?" Shelly asked, standing and zipping up her red jacket. "Do we wait?"

"We'll continue our investigation of this lake from the shore side. I'm leaving the canoe here. I hope that the sorcerers will think that we aren't here." As he gazed toward the dawning light on the lake, Colt picked up his pack. "We'll work slowly down the shore behind them and stay in the brush where we can because of the bright colors of our jackets. Chances are they're going to scour every bit of Moraine by canoe. That will take them a couple of hours and give us more time."

"And when they take the canoe back to the livery, what then?" Shelly asked, sliding on her knapsack.

"I'm sure they'll ask the attendant how many canoes there are and find one missing."

"That means they'll come back and start hunting for us onshore," she said, unhappy.

"Right. But that's two hours away. If we get lucky, we'll stay hidden and they won't be able to figure out where we are. That buys us more time, too."

Giving the dark waters a longing look, Shelly said, "Oh, how I wish the sphere was close and we could find it and then get out of here without them knowing anything."

Colt led her out of the brush and they moved along the shore. "Nothing in life is easy, Shelly. You know that."

"I know," she murmured, taking the lead. The light was getting brighter and brighter. It was easy to see the stones, the fallen limbs and branches along the shore. "If wishes were horses." She laughed softly.

Colt wanted things to be easy, too, for a lot of other reasons. Just knowing the sorcerers were on this lake, probably seven minutes ahead of them, sent alertness flowing through him. Shelly had said there was no way to combat a sorcerer except through love. When Colt thought about Shelly's form of protection against all sorcery, he found it hard to embrace. She'd never encountered a sorcerer until now and had never tested her theory. He trusted his own training now as never before.

If one of the sorcerers struck, Colt knew he would go after Shelly. Would his bubble of protection hold against such an attack? Colt wouldn't know until it happened. This made searching the shore even more important. Most of all, they had to remain hidden.

After another ten minutes of walking, Shelly pulled up. They had come to the curve in the lake. From their vantage point they could see the red canoe farther down to the south hugging the shoreline. She stood back and remained hidden by the trees. "There they are."

"Yes," Colt said, coming up and placing his arm around her shoulders. "They're trying to find us."

Shelly welcomed Colt's unexpected embrace and leaned against him. "My knees are shaking."

"I know." Colt looked into her upturned face, and his heart squeezed. A fierce love welled up through him. "It's going to be all right." He didn't really believe that, but he wanted her to believe it.

Closing her eyes, Shelly rested her head against his shoulder. "I just want this over with. I never realized just how horribly dangerous it was going to be." Pursing her lips, she added, "I wouldn't have done it, Colt. I wouldn't have shown up here hoping to meet you."

"Too late now," Colt said, pressing a chaste kiss on the top of her head. "We're okay, Shelly. Those dreams we had are real. The Great Spirit chose us for this. I don't know why, but we need to find this emerald. Let's keep looking for a vortex."

"I've never wanted to see two boulders sitting together as much as I do right now," she said in a fierce undertone. What was this gemstone sphere all about? Colt was right: curiosity drove them forward. She hoped it would be worth it because right now, their lives were on the line—literally.

Laughing softly, Colt released her. "I know what you're saying. So long as the sorcerer is in sight of us on this lake, we have to be shadows. Let's continue to walk the tree line. We can see the shore well enough and they certainly won't see us."

"Do you think they'll see our jackets?" Shelly asked in a worried tone.

Colt considered the question. She wore a red one and he wore a yellow one. The sun was coming up and they were on the west side of the lake. That meant as the sunlight poured above the line of mountains, it would hit them first. Right now, they were covered in deep shadows. "When the sun starts to bridge the mountains to the east of us, we'll take them off and stuff them into our day packs. I think we're safe enough for now. They're looking forward, not behind them. We'll stay far enough into the brush that if they do look around, they won't spot us."

"Good," Shelly said. "It's cold! Only after the sun comes over the mountains does it really start to warm up here."

Colt agreed. "Okay, let's move back into the woods a little more." Brush grew sporadically and they could thread in and around those areas. It gave good cover. The going was slow because plenty of limbs had fallen over the years due to heavy snowfall. They had to stay focused or else.

VICTOR STOOD ON THE WHARF, hands on hips. The man tasked with canoe rental was mollified as Victor handed him plenty of extra cash for the canoe they'd used. When they'd floated up to the dock, the man, a square-faced Scot named T. S. Mitchell, had blustered angrily at them. Their sincere-sounding apology had instantly mollified him.

"So, tell me," Victor said in his most charming manner, "are there any other canoes missing?"

"Aye, there is, sir. A green one."

"Are you sure?" Lothar demanded.

"Yes, sir, I am."

"I see," Victor murmured. He turned and looked out across the lake. The sun had risen and the temperature was warming. Moraine looked like a stunning turquoise jewel set amid the dark blue-gray granite and white-capped Rocky Mountains. At any other time, he'd have enjoyed the beauty of Banff, but not this morning.

Turning, he said to Lothar, "Let's go. I don't know about you, but that early-morning canoe trip has made me hungry. Ready for breakfast?"

Lothar nodded and said, "I'm hungry enough to eat a buffalo!"

Victor waved to the Scot. "Thank you."

"Sir?"

Victor halted. "Yes?"

"You know there's a grizzly bear alert out, don't you? We can't rent our canoes today because there's a sow grizzly with two cubs on the eastern side of the lake."

"Oh," Victor murmured, "I didn't know that."

"Yes, sir. And if you're planning on hiking in this area, that entire side of the lake is off-limits today. Sometimes this sow comes down to the lake hunting for newborn elk calves. And today is that day."

"Thanks for the warning," Victor said, lifting his hand to the Scot.

As they walked up the hill, Victor said, "That's an interesting twist, don't you think?"

"What? A bear down at this lake?"

"Yes. I know those *Taqe* are here. They were smart enough to dump the canoe and continue their search on foot." At the top of the hill overlooking the lake, Victor frowned. "The only question now is—where are they? Which way did they paddle before they hid the canoe?"

Lothar shrugged. "I haven't picked up anything on them."

"Of course not," Victor said, frowning. "They're warriors. They know how to cloak themselves and hide from us. There's no way for us to detect them."

Victor turned on his heel. "Come on, let's go to the parking lot and meet Jeff. He didn't find anyone on the highway because the *Taqe* are here at this lake. Let's go get him and eat breakfast here at the lodge."

Lothar nodded; he felt starved. "And then what, my lord?"

Moving toward the wooden lodge, Victor smiled. "I think the best way to find those two is to find that grizzly bear."

"What do you mean?" Lothar asked.

Rubbing his hands together, Victor said, "After breakfast, I'm going to ditch this body and go find that mother grizzly. We may not be able to find the *Taqe* but I'll guarantee you this—a bear can smell a human if they are downwind from them a mile away. I'll possess the bear and go hunt for them." He snickered, pleased with his plan. "It takes a hunter to find a hunter…"

"Stop!" Shelly threw out her hand. They stood about three feet inside the tree line on the eastern side of Moraine Lake. "A vortex!"

Colt came up to her side. "Yes, I can feel it, too. Let's approach."

Shelly moved ahead while Colt kept watch from the rear, constantly perusing the lake for the sorcerers. There were no other canoes on the lake and that confused Colt. It was a beautiful, clear day; why was nobody out paddling? That made him even more wary than before.

Pointing, Shelly said excitedly, "It's an androgynous vortex!"

Colt shifted his focus to where she was jabbing her index finger. He looked down at her. Her face was flushed, her eyes glimmering with excitement.

"Do you see those two boulders over there, too?" he asked.

"I don't know. I have to climb down the bank to see..." Shelly whispered. "This is it, Colt! I just know it." She pressed her hand over her heart.

Wary, Colt said, "Maybe."

"No, this is it."

"What will you do first?" Colt knew how he'd handle this, but Shelly had spent her life hunting vortexes. Besides, it focused her on something positive rather than the sorcerers hunting them.

"Walk into the vortex. Find out what kind of

portal it is or where it goes or what it's connected to."

"You might disappear," Colt said. "Are you prepared for that?"

"I am."

"Have you disappeared before in one?" Colt had and he knew it could be a parallel world that she'd step into.

"Yes. I scared my father to death one time. We were checking out an androgynous vortex in the Northern Territories when I disappeared."

"How long were you gone? Where did you go?"

"It was about five minutes before I reappeared, but it felt as though I was gone a lot longer than that. My poor dad was beside himself with worry. He knew enough not to step into the vortex himself. So he waited, but it was hard on him."

Colt could see why. "Where did the portal open up to?"

"It was an interesting one," she said. "Are you familiar with the Australian Aborigines and their Dream Time?"

"Yes, but tell me what you know," Colt said.

"*Dream Time* is another term for a whole bunch of androgynous vortex sites around the world. The Aboriginal people know where these vortexes are located in Australia. They enter the vortex, the door opens and whisks them into the fourth dimension.

They can travel along these energy ley-line highways to other places. The androgynous vortexes are placed far apart, yet they help make travel easy. This way metaphysical knowledge has been traded and shared with mystics the world over from ancient times to the present," Shelly said eagerly. "Not only that, the mystics of the different countries shared their symbols, artwork and legends with one another. No matter where you go around the world, you will see identical symbols from one continent to another. And this is how much of it happened. Isn't that exciting?"

Colt absorbed her enthusiasm. "It's interesting. So, this vortex might be a door to that inner highway that the elders traverse?"

"I won't know until I step into it." She reached out and squeezed his hand. "Now, if I disappear, don't panic, okay? I'll be back. I know how to enter and leave a vortex portal, so just be patient." She stared up into Colt's turbulent blue eyes, seeing worry in them. Reaching up, she wrapped her arms around his shoulders. Her lips impulsively met his and she didn't care that this distracted Colt. She needed to kiss him. There was danger entering this type of a vortex and she didn't want to leave without telling him goodbye.

Stunned by Shelly's sudden kiss, Colt groaned and wrapped his arms around her curved body. The moment her lips brushed his mouth, they parted. She tasted sweet, as only Shelly could. Taking her full weight, Colt anchored her and breathed in the scent of her riot of red hair that swirled around at her sudden move. He hungrily pressed his lips to her soft and exploring mouth. He felt her smile beneath his and relaxed for the first time since they'd begun this quest. Her tongue moved boldly across his lower lip. The jolt of electricity dove down through him to his lower body. The world ceased to exist as Colt absorbed her in every possible way.

The firmness of her breasts pressed against his chest. Her arms were lean and strong, holding him close. The beat of her heart reminded him of a little bird. Her lips wreaked a fire that exploded through him. As her tongue tentatively touched his, Colt lost all contact with the world outside. The movement was so sensuous that he felt his knees grow weak with need—of her.

Breathing raggedly, Shelly pulled away, her hands on his shoulders. She looked up into his hooded blue eyes and smiled. "I'll walk in the vortex but I'll be back." She tried to sound confident. Shelly released Colt, spun on the heel of her boot and walked forward with authority toward the invisible vortex. And then, she was gone.

Colt felt the portal open and close. He could see the white and gold energy and the door. Shelly

disappeared in an instant, gone to somewhere unknown. He loved Shelly. He loved her as he'd never
loved another woman. It took everything he had to
wait for her. Colt knew medicine men who had gone
through portals on the reservation—never to come
back. It was always a dicey proposition and he tried
to control his anxiety, to continue his high state of
alert.

Just as he wrestled with Shelly's absence, he
sensed a sorcerer nearby. Was he in a canoe? On
foot? Colt wasn't sure. But he did feel that the
sorcerer stalked them in earnest. This time, their
adversary intended to find them.

Chapter 16

Shelly stepped into the vortex energy. The moment she placed her left boot on the black boulder and her right boot on the white boulder, she felt an incredible shift of energy and closed her eyes. Where would the vortex take her?

Her lips still tingled from Colt's kiss and her heart swelled with incredible love for him. No matter what happened on this dangerous journey, she had met the man of her dreams. Her past relationships no longer had a hold on her. Colt was a trustworthy person, a man she could love without fear of being used or manipulated. With that emo-

tional energy swirling about her, Shelly did not fight
the unseen but felt movement around her. This was
a familiar sensation, which calmed any anxiety she
might have had.

As she stood there, her knees slightly softened,
hands at her sides, a warmth embraced her. The
sense of motion ceased.

Open your eyes, Shelly.

The mental command startled her and she opened
her eyes. There was a white gauze everywhere she
looked. She heard the command but saw no one.

*I've come for the emerald sphere. Do you have
it?* she asked telepathically as she turned around to
glance behind her. The whitish filaments reminded
her of the high cirrus clouds in the sky. They would
rotate clockwise at a slow pace and then turn in the
other direction.

She began to see someone materialize about six
feet away from her. It was a woman with slightly
tilted green eyes. Shelly didn't recognize her. She
was tall, with seaweed surrounding her lithe form.
Her feet were encased in brightly colored coral. Her
hair seemed composed of fine, thin seaweed flowing
in an unseen channel of energy. This was not a
human being. Luckily, Shelly had come across any
number of alien beings, gods and goddesses in other
portals she'd explored over the years. It was the
female's large green, slanted eyes, however, that

calmed her. Love and nurturing radiated from this being.

I am Niru, daughter of the Ocean.

Bowing her head in deference to the being, Shelly said, *I am honored by your presence. Are you from the oceans of our Mother?* Shelly felt rather than saw the goddess's smile. It sent radiant tingles of joy through her.

My true home is on a beach in a place you call the South Island of New Zealand. I was born there many millions of your years ago. My work is to keep the water of this planet clean and alive. My workers are the dolphins and whale people who maintain a peaceful harmony so that Mother Earth may survive the onslaught from human beings. When you see a rainbow, that is a sign I am nearby.

Shelly felt as if she were standing in the flow of the ocean although she could not see it. *Thank you for being who you are. Humans have fouled the water on this Earth and I know there are many of us who are trying to stop this.* A tremendous sense of water flowed in vast, slow currents all around Shelly. Was this a portal into Niru's watery oceanic kingdom?

Yes, you are within a chamber of my home near New Zealand, Niru signaled. *Do not be fearful, for you will not drown. This chamber is a door to those who want to work with me. I have any number of vortex portals around the world for humans who care about the health of our oceans. You will always find these doors near ponds, lakes, streams, oceans or rivers. Anyone who wants to work with me simply gives a gift to the water, calls my name, and I will come.*

Shelly smiled. *This is a wonderful way to work with you, my lady. Are you the caretaker of the emerald sphere we seek?*

Niru lifted her arms, which were draped in kelp. *A long time ago an Incan priestess came to the South Island of New Zealand. She found the cave where I was born. Praying, she asked me to come to her and keep the emerald sphere. I said I would. One day, the priestess told me, a woman would appear, a woman born to touch the sphere and help it to its next destination. I promised I would do all I could so I sent you and Colt the same dream. You both came here to connect with me.*

Shelly was amazed by this revelation. How could that Incan priestess have known she would even exist or follow through? *Dear Niru, if you feel I am the right woman, may I have the sphere now? We are ready to receive it for we want nothing but peace upon this planet.*

It is with great pleasure and anticipation that I gift you with the sphere. Be aware, my daughter, that this sphere symbolizes courage.

Shelly saw the seaweed arms flow together in front of her. Emerald-green and turquoise water flowed around Niru to give her a long, lithe shape. Shelly's gaze narrowed upon the kelp hands of the sea goddess. For a moment, nothing happened. Then, the sphere appeared in the cupped leaves of the seaweed. Within moments, it became more and more solid. As it formed, she saw within the depths of the emerald gold emanations shooting out from all around it like rays from a blazing, glorious sun. Gasping, Shelly felt the energy of the sphere as it fully materialized within Niru's hands.

My daughter, Niru warned, *as I place this sphere in your hands, you will be taken back to your time and place. Be warned that danger awaits you. Only love can save you. Remember that....*

Thank you, my lady. I appreciate your care of this sphere for all of our relations on this planet we love so much. She reached out with her left hand. Her heart pounded with excitement, as the sphere left the cupped hands of kelp leaves and drifted toward her. The sphere settled into her palm. It was heavy, much more so than she had expected. Curling her fingers around it, she said, *Thank you, dear Niru.* She touched her heart with her right hand and bowed her head in deference to the ancient sea goddess.

Go in peace and light, my daughter, Niru signaled.

In moments, Niru dissolved and only the white, slow-moving filaments of light floated around Shelly once more. With the incredible power and love throbbing through her body, Shelly realized for the first time the sphere's strength. No wonder the sorcerers wanted it!

She closed her eyes and shifted back to her world, to where she was standing on those two boulders on the bank of Moraine Lake. Niru's warning haunted her: they were in danger. They could die….

COLT ANXIOUSLY WATCHED as Shelly materialized. Her booted feet were solidly placed on the two boulders. In her left hand was an incredibly beautiful and powerful emerald sphere. She had found it!

Before Colt had time to celebrate, he heard the roar of a huge animal behind him. As he turned abruptly, his eyes widened. There was a mother silver-tipped grizzly bear charging toward him with two cubs at her heels! Colt tensed. On the Navajo reservation he'd never had an encounter with bears of any kind. More than his own life, he had to protect Shelly. But how? The grizzly bear lumbered toward him at frightening speed. Her mouth was open, saliva dripping from the sides, her teeth bared.

There!

Colt leaned down. A soggy limb lay off the bank of the lake, about six feet long and as thick as a man's wrist. Gripping it, Colt wrenched it out of the water. The grizzly shifted course from him to where Shelly materialized.

No! Colt whirled around and shouted at the bear to get her attention. Scrambling up from the smooth, slippery rocks, limb between his hands, he ran to interdict the raging, angry mother bear. His mind spun as he went to confront the nine-hundred-pound grizzly. Of all things, he'd never expected to be attacked by a bear!

Digging into the slope of the bank with the toes of his boots, Colt leaped up to the grassy earth above. The two cubs were running hard to keep up with their mother. They, too, were ferocious. How could he keep all three of them from attacking Shelly?

Taking a stand, Colt stood between the charging grizzlies and Shelly down at the lakeshore. Breathing hard, air exploding from his mouth, Colt anchored himself. Less than fifty feet lay between him and the enormous angry mother bear. Colt felt like a fly next to an out-of-control truck hurtling down the slope at him.

As the bear charged, her mouth open, the roar vibrating through Colt, he lifted the limb. When he was a child, he used to herd sheep through the mesas where coyotes would stalk the animals. There, he would pick up a long limb and charge the coyotes.

His father had always said that a whack on the nose would make the animal run away. The nose of any wild animal was their weak point, the most sensitive spot on the body.

Lifting the branch over his head, Colt swung down hard just as the bear made a flying lunge directly at him. His arms took the brunt of the solid hit. He'd aimed the limb right at the mother bear's sensitive nose. The clash of hurtling animal against the power and force of his strike snapped the limb in half with a powerful cracking sound.

The bear slammed hard to the ground, roaring in pain. With her huge, long claws, she pawed again and again at her badly bleeding nose.

Colt gasped and leaped to the side as the bear fell only three feet away from him. He didn't have time to watch what the mother would do. Two cubs, easily weighing four hundred pounds each, charged him instead.

Whirling around, the limb half the length it was before, Colt struck out at the first cub. He hit it hard in the head. The animal bawled and tumbled backward.

The second cub growled and charged. Both hands gripping the club, Colt struck out again. With deadly accuracy, he managed to direct the broken tip of the limb to the cub's nose. It, too, screamed in pain, tumbled backward over and over again, pawing wildly at its bleeding nose.

Breathing hard, Colt risked a look over his shoulder. Shelly was completely back! She'd just stepped off the boulders and turned to look up the slope at him. Her eyes were wide with disbelief.

He jerked his attention back to the bears, noticing that the mother's nose bled heavily. She had backed off, swiping repeatedly at her wounded snout. The two cubs had scampered back behind her. He stood, panting and waiting for their next charge. The more he looked into the bear's small eyes, the more he saw the flat blackness. Something was wrong, but Colt couldn't understand what was going on.

"Colt, come here!" Shelly cried out.

Keeping the club in hand, Colt turned and ran down the slope. He skidded on the stones as he came to a halt in front of her. "Are you all right?" he demanded, out of breath.

"Yes, yes. Are you okay?" She reached out, terrified.

"I'm fine, but we're in trouble. Those bears could charge again. We can't outrun them, Shelly. And we don't have a canoe to escape to the lake." He turned, gazing up the slope. The mother bear was shaking her head, still nursing her injured muzzle.

"Oh, God," Shelly cried, pointing at the bear.

Colt's eyes became slits. He saw a huge black cloud come shooting out of the top of the mother bear's head. In seconds, the animal turned around and started lumbering off at a trot toward the tree line with her cubs in tow.

"The sorcerer!" Shelly screamed. What she did next was without thought, only a survival reflex. Something drove her to throw her right arm around Colt. In her left hand Shelly held the flashing golden and emerald sphere between them, at heart level. A huge sonic boom occurred, as if a military jet had broken the sound barrier right over their heads. The ground and air trembled violently in the wake of the earsplitting sound.

Colt hauled Shelly into his arms. She kept the emerald against his chest where his heart lay. Colt felt an incredible seismic shift of energy around him. He had already thrown up a protective barrier against their attacker. The sorcerer in the black, roiling cloud was nearly upon them. Colt knew the sorcerer was hidden somewhere in that thunderstorm cloud moving swiftly toward them. The sorcerer would do anything to get the sphere from Shelly.

Colt held her tightly against himself and turned his back toward the sorcerer who was diving down at them.

As soon as he'd done that, another powerful shift occurred. To Colt, it sounded like a second military jet had just broken the sound barrier right on top of them. The earth quivered violently beneath his feet, and he felt the vibration through every cell of his body. Shelly clung to him. Colt automatically closed his eyes. He gritted his teeth and waited for the malevolent attack.

When it didn't happen, Colt jerked his head up and looked above them. His eyes widened as a huge green bubble surrounded them. What was going on? Jerking his gaze upward, he watched as the angry sorcerer kept charging down at them with full weight and fury. And then, something happened that Colt hadn't anticipated.

He heard a keening shriek. A long, wailing cry of a man in utter shock. The thunderous, roiling black cloud that hid the sorcerer halted a few feet above them. He held Shelly hard against him. If anyone was going to die, it would be him. Shelly had to survive! He loved her with his life.

And then, he felt Shelly lift her head.

"The sphere is protecting us!" she cried.

No wonder everything looked greenish to Colt. He couldn't figure out what had happened until Shelly had cried out. Indeed, a warm sensation pulsed between them where the emerald rested. The precious sphere had saved them from the sorcerer's attack.

Within seconds, Colt saw two smaller black clouds join the larger one above the green bubble. All three sorcerers had possessed the bears. They moved around the bubble seeking entry.

"They can't reach us!" Colt rasped, grateful for the protection.

Just when he felt sure of their safety, Yellow Teeth came from the sky toward them like a rocket. Instantly, he went on internal guard and girded himself for the coming attack. The Skin Walker's mouth opened, lifting away from teeth as he pounced.

Again, there was a loud cracking sound, a tooth-jarring reverberation as the Skin Walker struck the bubble with full force. Colt watched in amazement as the witch slammed into the green energy, causing a blinding explosion of light. Suddenly, the Skin Walker disappeared in a flash. He had been killed by touching the light of the emerald sphere. Finally, his nemesis was dead.

But Colt couldn't let himself gloat or cheer. The other three thunderstorms of terrifying black clouds continued to hover inches above the green energy. They seemed to realize the energy, if touched, would kill them, too. Colt pulled Shelly closer, hoping his deepest fears could now be put to rest.

VICTOR GUERRA HOWLED in frustration. If he touched that greenish bubble of protection, it would turn him from *Tupay* into a *Taqe*. While Lothar knew this, too, Jeff, no doubt curious and new to the world of the *Tupay,* touched the energy of the bubble.

"No!" Victor screamed. "Don't let it touch you!"

Too late! Jeff bounced off the bubble's shimmering gold-and-green surface like a golf ball ricocheting off a wall.

Angry, Victor snarled to Lothar, "Go get him! See if it's changed him!"

Glaring at the bubble and the two *Taqe* within it, who were clearly frightened, Victor cursed once more. For whatever reason, this damned sphere was going to protect these two. There was no way to get to them. No matter what he did now, the sphere was clearly on the side of the *Taqe*. Victor knew he had to leave.

Turning, he noticed Lothar kneeling over Jeff.

"How is he?" Victor demanded. In the fourth dimension they were in human form once more. To someone in the third dimension, they appeared as dark and massive thunderstorms.

"I'm okay. Really I am…" Jeff muttered, shaking his head.

Lothar crouched at Jeff's shoulder. The younger spirit held his head in his hands, bent over and clearly stunned.

"You stupid fool!" Victor barked at Jeff. "You don't ever touch anything around a *Taqe*. It's deadly to us. Didn't you see that Skin Walker get zapped? His soul is dead!"

Jeff nodded and felt shaken to his core. "Y-yes, my lord. I'm sorry, I didn't know," he mumbled, his insides feeling like so much jelly. Odd emotions circuited through him. "I feel like I touched an electric line and got zapped."

Lothar patted his shoulder. "It's okay. Don't worry."

Victor glared at the fleeing grizzly bears up on the slope. They had trotted away to the safety of the forest, no worse for wear. Animals did not suffer the fate of humans. Their silver cords did not get severed and they always lived after being possessed. When Colt had struck the nose of the mother bear, Victor had felt pain directly as never before. Who knew the *Taqe* would pick up a limb and hit his nose with it? The resourcefulness of the Warriors for the Light never ceased to amaze him.

"Let's go," he said. "There's no sense in staying around here. Jeff, get over to the energy hospital. You will need care to heal from your injuries."

Victor watched Lothar help Jeff to his feet, his arm around his waist to help the young *Tupay* stand. With a flourish of his hand, he sent all three of them back to the fortress.

"THEY'RE GONE!" Colt growled, relief tunneling through him. He scanned the area to be certain. He was still holding Shelly, and the green bubble of protection continued to shimmer around them.

"Are you sure?" she asked.

"I don't see them," Colt told her. "And I don't sense them hanging around here. No, they're gone." Gazing down at Shelly, he asked in an urgent voice, "Are you okay? You aren't hurt, are you?"

Just the concern in Colt's voice helped ground her. She clutched the sphere in her left hand between them so tightly her fingers ached. "I'm fine. Truly, I'm fine. Thank you for protecting me, Colt. I came out of that portal and I saw the bears charging you. I was never so scared…." She choked and her eyes filled with tears and his face blurred.

Just then, Colt sensed someone materializing behind them up on the bank. With Shelly still protected in his arms, Colt looked up to see a very old man and woman in white robes.

"Who are they?" Shelly asked, her voice hoarse with fear.

Colt was aware that the green bubble of protection had disappeared. And just as suddenly, the green sphere flew from Shelly's grasp and into the hands of the woman with the silver hair. What was going on?

The bearded old man, a crooked wooden staff in his right hand, called, "Be at peace. We are your friends. I am called Adaire. This is my wife, Alaria. We are going to take you to a place of safety. It is time you knew more about the emerald sphere."

Before Colt could open his mouth, the man,

whose eyes blazed blue, lifted his staff and pointed it at them. There was a loud boom and a flash of bright, blinding light. Without thinking, Colt gripped Shelly to him. He heard her scream. And then he closed his eyes and held her tightly as he felt swift movement around them.

Chapter 17

Colt opened his eyes as soon as their surroundings seemed to have stilled. They were standing on a red-tiled balcony overlooking a tropical jungle. Either from bewilderment or uneasiness, they broke apart and Shelly went to look around. As they took stock of their new environment, the old woman with white braids materialized before them.

"Be at peace. I am Alaria from the Village of the Clouds," she greeted with a warm smile. "You have saved this emerald sphere and we are grateful. The *Tupay* sorcerers are gone. They will not come back to bother you. We have brought you here to the Vesica

Pisces Foundation just outside Quito, Ecuador. There are people here who will tell you all about the emerald you have found. Blessings." She raised her hand and gave them a benediction before disappearing.

The calls of parrots and howler monkeys came from the nearby jungle. Above them, thin, wispy clouds and pale blue sky met their gaze. Hearing footsteps from the other side of the opened doors, Colt lifted his head. Who was coming? And how had they arrived in South America?

"CONGRATULATIONS!" Calen said to Colt and Shelly. She smiled warmly as they all sat together in their Ecuadorian headquarters. "Now you know the whole story about the emerald sphere. What an incredible challenge you've had in finding this sphere. We're grateful to both of you."

"Did you worry that with the last mission's failure, the spheres had abandoned you?" Shelly asked.

"Yes," Calen said, frowning. "Before this event, I would get a dream of where the next one could be found. After we lost Robert Cramer, I never received the dream of where the next emerald sphere was located. Alaria and Adaire, who are the leaders of the Village of the Clouds, our *Taqe* stronghold in the fourth dimension, were not allowed to get involved.

Instead, the sphere's spirit sent you two a dream. It had chosen you." Pressing her hand to her breast, Calen said, "I'm so relieved. We learn as we go with these spheres. The good news is that they do talk with one another."

"Yes," Reno added, grinning. "We're in good hands even if you never get another dream, Calen. We'll find the next one."

"I hope so," Calen responded.

"Could it be that because of what happened, the spirit of the spheres knows the best way to choose the people for the next one?" Colt asked.

"It looks that way," Reno agreed.

"And that's fine with us," Calen said. "We just need the next one now."

"I feel that the sphere will probably contact the person it needs," Shelly said. "It's just a hunch."

"Probably a correct one," Reno said. "We'll have to wait and see. Alaria was notified and told to contact you once the sphere was given to you by Niru, the sea goddess."

Colt nodded. "I know you're surprised that Guerra possessed a grizzly bear, but in my Navajo traditions sorcerers deliberately possess a coyote. They're known as Skin Walkers and our people are terrified of them."

"Still, this is a first. None of our other teams had to deal with animals as part of the *Tupay* strategy," Reno said.

"We want to congratulate the two of you. This is wonderful. The sphere is already back at the *Taqe* village for safekeeping," Calen said.

Shelly sighed. She was still coming down from the entire mystical journey. "I kept thinking Guerra would attack us again and try to steal the sphere back."

"What we're learning from these missions about the spheres," Reno said, "is that once the sphere makes a connection with the heart of the rescuer, no matter whether it's *Tupay* or *Taqe,* it will go with them. The one we lost didn't have the opportunity or time to create that connection with our people. Which is why Guerra could steal it."

"How are you ever going to get it back?" Colt asked. "We understood that no *Taqe* can ever enter the fortress of the *Tupay* in the fourth dimension."

"That's right," Calen said. "We can't. And we still don't know how we can rescue it."

"If the foundation can find the other spheres, that will give you six out of the seven," Shelly remarked.

"Yes," Calen said. "But we need all of them in order to complete the necklace. That will allow Ana to wear it to make the vibrational or resonance changes to our planet so we can head for the light and get out of this heavy, dark *Tupay* energy."

"Dealing with Guerra was life-and-death," Colt said, his hands folded on the table. He gazed over at Shelly, who had faint dark circles beneath her eyes.

"There's no doubt the skills of both of you were the key," Reno said, giving them a nod of deference. "And once you two have had a chance to rest up, we're going to ask each of you to write up a detailed report on your experiences. Plus, we'd like a manual on vortexes that we'll keep here at the foundation." Reno smiled a little. "And along that line, we'd like to offer both of you a job to work for us here at the foundation. None of us know that much about vortexes. We need you to train us. We can't assume that vortexes won't be involved in finding the other spheres. You're the experts. What do you say?"

"Oh, gosh," Shelly said, giving Colt a worried look. "I don't know…"

"We've hired all the mission specialists after they've returned," Reno said in way of explanation. "Each of you brings a skill, understanding and expertise to us. Colt, your knowledge of sorcerers possessing an animal is new to us, but not to you. We are constantly building a broader base of information for those who come here for training. What you know is important," Reno said. "And we'd like to extend a career opening here at the foundation for each of you. We'll be offering you two hundred and fifty thousand dollars for finding the sphere. And the same amount per year to be in tenured positions with our foundation. We expect you to write papers, maybe a book and to teach here at the institute."

Stunned, Colt ran the amount of money through his mind. That was a quarter of a million dollars a year! He stared across the table at Reno. No question, the man was Native American with his copper-toned skin and rich brown eyes. His long, straight black hair flowed across his massive shoulders. "Yes, I would like to do that." Colt knew his father would be disappointed, but would understand. At last, he felt for the first time, he was on a path that was more in line with his spiritual skills and knowledge. His heart opened as he realized the dream of loving Shelly was now possible. Did she want to be a part of his life?

"Are you going to accept their offer?" Colt asked, searching Shelly's face for answers.

"Yes, I am. We're a good team, Colt." Her eyes grew soft and warm as she held his gaze.

"And on that note, we can table any other discussions on this mission for now," Calen said, rising. "We have two bedrooms, with a door between, that we want you to take here at our home. Stay, heal and rest up for as long as you want. When you two feel it's time to get back to work here with us, come and let us know. Reno, do you want to show them to their quarters?"

"Let's go." Reno gestured for them to follow.

While a bit worried over how she would react, Colt held out his hand to Shelly. Would she take it?

To his relief, she gave him a shy smile and slid her hand into his. His heart pounded with hope—hope of a future together with her. A wild joy grew inside him as they traversed the mahogany hall behind Reno. The lights along the corridor showed off the beautiful dark, reddish wood. At the stairs, he led them up to a third floor. Just the idea that they would be close to one another made Colt's soul sing.

Reno stopped halfway down the hall. At the other end was a large arched window and the light flowed brightly into the area. "Here you are. We eat dinner at 8:00 p.m. It's 10:00 a.m. now. Why don't you get some sleep in the meantime?"

"Sounds good," Shelly said, thanking Reno. "We'll see you for dinner."

Colt watched Reno move like a ghost down the hall, soundless despite his bulk. When he felt Shelly's hazel gaze upon him, he turned to her. Everything about his life seemed possible now, even happiness. Especially happiness. "What do you want?"

Touching his cheek, she whispered, "First, I want a long, wonderful bath. I need to fully relax and clean up from our ordeal."

"After that?" He swallowed hard, waiting for her answer.

Her lips curved. "I want to come over to your room and make love."

Colt hadn't expected this invitation, but it told him she was serious about him. "I'll be waiting for you," Colt said. The mere idea of Shelly's soft, beautiful form next to his was nearly overwhelming. He opened the door to her suite.

Shelly gave him a quick kiss on the cheek and disappeared inside.

Colt stood out in the hall feeling a week's worth of exhaustion tunneling through him. For the first time, he realized they were safe. Really safe. The sphere was safe, too. He opened his door and stepped in. His heart swelled with anticipation, with so many emotions he'd suppressed. Soon, he and Shelly would be together, really together.

THE SCENT OF JASMINE filled Shelly's nostrils as she brought the sash of the long emerald silk robe around her waist. The fabric was a delicious sensation against her clean skin. She walked out of the bathroom and into her living area. The suite had two rooms. She loved the palms in large, colorful ceramic pots in either corner of the outer room next to the windows. There was a mahogany desk, a computer, a chair, a couch and a flat-screened television up above the mantel of the fireplace.

As much as she wanted to luxuriate in this beautiful suite, she wanted to be with Colt. She moved her fingers through her recently washed hair, trying to stave off any lingering nervousness. She gave a soft knock on the inner door but heard nothing. It had been nearly an hour since they'd parted. Easing the door open, she hesitantly stepped into the room. An overstuffed sofa and chair sat at one end, a similar layout to her suite.

"Colt?" she called softly. Shelly shut the door, puzzled. Where was he? The door to his bedroom stood ajar. Standing for a moment, her heart pounding with anticipation, she waited. She called out his name again. No answer. Was he in the shower? If he was, he wouldn't hear her.

She padded across the red-and-beige tiles and halted at the bedroom door. Hand upon the frame, she gazed toward the king-size bed in the center of the room. There, Colt was fast asleep. The yellow sheet had been pulled up to his waist. He lay on his stomach, hands beneath the pillow. There was something incredibly vulnerable about Colt in sleep that she'd never seen in him when he was awake. Her heart sang as she went over to his bed. She could see he was naked beneath the sheet. She appreciated the long, lean lines of his body, the thick male muscling across his shoulders and down the deeply indented line of his spine. What an urge she felt to touch him.

Shelly told herself that she could wait. Allowing the silk robe to slip off her shoulders, she laid it across the end of the bed. The yellow sheet brought out the copper color of his skin. She could hear him breathing deeply and slowly in sleep. His hair had been washed and needed to be combed. Shelly wanted to do that. Every inch of his body was something she wanted to explore with her hands and lips. But not now. Exhaustion pulled at her, too. Slipping into the bed, Shelly brought up the sheet. And then, she lay on her side inches away from Colt. First, sleep. As she closed her eyes, she inhaled the male fragrance that was only Colt. Reaching out, she slid her hand across his tightly muscled shoulder. The loads he'd carried for both of them in Canada were finally removed, she thought, closing her eyes.

As she lay there, the melodic songs of tropical birds outside the huge, arched window were muted. How wonderful it was to lie here with the man she loved so fiercely and have the songs of Ecuadorian birds to lull her to sleep. As her fingers came to rest on his shoulder, a soft smile curved Shelly's mouth. *Safe.* They were safe. That was all that counted. Safe to explore one another finally. Safe to love one another without fear of Guerra attacking them. A soft sigh slipped from between her parted lips. Sleep came quickly.

COLT AWOKE SLOWLY. He was cocooned in the wonderful world of sleep. While his eyes were still closed, his senses slowly came to life. The first sounds he heard were birds singing in the trees outside the window. The melodies were long and he enjoyed them. Then, he inhaled a feminine scent. This was new. He dragged his eyes open, seeing that he now lay on his left side—facing Shelly. Colt hungrily absorbed her sleeping form next to him. Only inches separated them. And she was naked, the yellow sheet revealing the contour of her hip and her long legs hidden beneath the languid folds.

His heart began a slow pounding that tore the sleep away from him. Was this another torrid dream? In the past days in Canada, Colt had dreamed about Shelly every night. He'd dream of waking up and finding her just like this—in his bed, naked, her beautiful breasts revealed and begging him to touch and kiss them. Dream or reality? He wasn't sure because his exhaustion had been so deep. His mind and body had pleaded for healing, for uninterrupted rest. Looking up, he saw that the sunlight had moved a great deal from the time he'd gone to bed. It was now late afternoon.

His gaze drifted back to Shelly's sleeping features. Her red hair was in mild disarray around her face and shoulders. One hand stretched outward from her pillow in his direction, the other hand rested against her naked breasts. Like a rich, sumptuous feast, Colt lay quietly absorbing the beauty of Shelly as a woman. Her freckles provided a coverlet

across her white skin. He stared at them like a
starving animal. Her mouth was full and the natural
upward curve at the corners made Colt smile to
himself. Shelly was such a positive person. Everything in her life was half-full, never half-empty as
he'd seen his own life. Lying so close and listening
to her softened breathing, Colt felt that darkness
within him dissipate once and for all. No longer did
he have to be a bastion of strength. If she loved him,
he could reveal his more vulnerable side to her. He
wouldn't have to keep his shields of protection up
all the time.

Colt eased up on his elbow. Though his fingers
were itching to touch her, he hesitated. Did he have
the courage to dream this new dream with Shelly in
it? Looking at her sleeping features, the soft arch of
her red eyebrows, the long lashes touching her
freckled cheeks, Colt knew in his heart she was all
he would ever want. With Shelly at his side, he felt
incredibly strong and hopeful. Truly, she was his
dream come true.

Unable to wait any longer, Colt eased his arm
around her waist and gently drew her against his
hardening body. As he moved her forward, her
lashes fluttered. And then, she opened her eyes and
he drowned in the glorious hazel—green, brown
and gold—of her drowsy gaze.

"Woman of my heart," he whispered. Leaning

down, Colt placed a soft, welcoming kiss against her parted lips. Closing his eyes, Colt heard and felt her moan. Shelly's arms enfolded him. When her breasts, warm and full, pressed against his chest, he groaned with utter pleasure. Their mouths became hungry and exploratory. The songs of the tropical birds provided a natural backdrop as he brought her fully against him in every way. Their hips met. He inhaled sharply as she moved provocatively against his hardness. There was such a sweet, natural reaction to Shelly.

"Colt…" Shelly whispered against his strong, seeking lips, "I love you…"

Turning her so that she sprawled across him, her body resting warmly upon his, Colt framed her face. They lay naked upon one another. He saw the drowsy look replaced by a sensual gold fire in the depths of her half-opened eyes. "I love you with all my heart and soul. I never want more than you. I want us to walk this life—together."

Wet lips curving softly, Shelly leaned closer. "I fell in love with you in Canada. You were willing to give your life for mine when Guerra attacked us." Kissing him slowly and thoroughly, Shelly lifted her head and held his dark blue eyes, hooded with desire. "When you turned me in your arms and placed your back toward Guerra, I knew your courage, Colt." Shelly lifted her hand and threaded her fingers through the sleek black strands of his short hair. "I was so scared. What you did makes me cry, my sweetheart."

Staring into her tear-filled eyes, Colt felt the tingling whisper of her fingertips across his scalp, the heat of her flesh against his, the soft smile of her mouth. "I would die for you, Shelly. Then and now. I can't see life without you being in it. You are my sunshine." He looked toward the shafts of afternoon light slanting into his suite. Colt moved his fingers through her silky hair. Each time he moved a strand across her shoulders, it would change color from copper to burgundy and then flash with gold highlights. "You are so beautiful."

Moving her hips suggestively, Shelly gave a throaty laugh as his fingers wreaked pleasure across her scalp. "We deserve one another, Colt." All her past wounds by men, her bad choices, were behind her. This was a new start with a man who wanted to support her dreams and aspirations. "I want to share my life with you here in Ecuador. I want to love you. Now…"

Without a word, she sat up and positioned her hips so that she could allow him entrance into her wet, ready body. Hands upon his chest, Shelly held his predatory gaze. As she lowered herself upon him, her lashes shuttered closed, her fingers dug into the tensing strength of his chest muscles. A gasp escaped her as she felt his hands come to rest upon her hips. He surged into her, and a cry of joy escaped her lips. Her world exploded with so many rainbow hues that she lost herself within them and absorbed his love for her.

The moments became hot, wet and wild as she moved down against his hips. Each thrust created liquid heat that ebbed and flowed through her lower body. When his lips closed over one nipple and then the other, Shelly sobbed with pleasure. His hands moved with such tenderness as they followed the curve of her breasts. She wanted to cry with the beauty of their love. His lips explored her neck, her jaw and finally came to rest upon her mouth. Colt sat up, his knees against her spine, his hands moving across her body in seductive exploration of every curve. His hands tantalized her shoulders, outlining her collarbones and then drifting down around her breasts. Shelly came undone.

He lay back down as if sensing her orgasm, his hands firm against her hips. She rode him as she would ride a wild, galloping stallion. Her fingers dug into his chest, a cry lurched from her parting lips as an explosion erupted from deep within her. Frozen in the splendor of the moment, she felt Colt moving his hips to create an even more intense reaction to the ongoing, flowing orgasm. And then, Shelly felt him stiffen, and groan like a wild animal.

The heat, their love, their bodies, his hands gripping her hips, it all became a rainbow of scintillating beauty.

Afterward, Shelly lay against Colt's body, exhausted. She gently touched his cheek, her head resting in the crook of his right shoulder, brow pressed against his jaw. "That was," she said, "wild…wonderful…"

Eyes closed, all Colt wanted was to absorb Shelly against him. He ran his fingers lingeringly down her lovely, long spine. "I knew we'd be good together. For one another…"

"We're going to have to do this often, Colt." She laughed.

Looking into her sparkling hazel eyes, dancing with gold in their depths, he said, "Oh, yes. Very often." They melted into mutual laughter as they held one another.

Colt continued to caress Shelly's curved back, her spine and flared hips. He liked the way their legs tangled with one another. Shelly was sleek and rounded. She was soft in so many places where he was hard and angled. The delicious aftermath of their lovemaking was rich and filled with their breathing, their kisses and exploration of one another.

Shelly eased up just enough to catch his gaze. "All I want, Colt, is you. I have always dreamed of a man with courage who would share my life. You are that man…."

Chapter 18

"We just got word from Grandmother Alaria at the Village of the Clouds," Reno told them at the breakfast table out on the patio the next morning. "The Sanskrit word carved into the sphere you found was *courage*."

Shelly's brows arched. "Oh, perfect!" She gave Colt, who sat at her right arm, a look of pride. "That fits, doesn't it? You had to deal with fear every day of Yellow Teeth taking possession of you. That took a lot of courage, Colt."

"That fits." Colt shared a warm look with Shelly. "And you had the courage to help find the emerald even though once you knew the risks, you didn't run. I believe the sphere's intent was for us to be courageous despite our fears." He smiled a little more. "And we were."

"Going after these spheres is always about life or death," Reno said.

"Speaking of the spheres," Calen said, worried, "I didn't have a dream last night about where the next one would be located."

Reno reached out and patted his wife's hand. "And that tells us a higher, more evolved energy is involved now." He gazed at Shelly and Colt. "And even though you didn't know what was going on, you trusted the power and the instructions given you. Both of you showed up at Banff where the sphere was located."

Calen smiled. "I sense that the other spheres will somehow choose people to go seek them out."

"But, like this one," Reno said, "we won't know about it or when it will happen or who is involved until they contact us as Colt and Shelly did."

"Right," Calen murmured, then brightened. "One thing we know is to have faith in the unseen process. This is a test for us and, in particular, me. I need to have faith that the spheres and their higher purpose are in better hands."

"Does that mean that the other spheres will contact someone else by sending a dream?" Colt asked.

Opening her hands, Calen said, "I don't know. I feel what we need to do is hold the energy, the expectation that the next one will be found and that the person or people will then be guided to us after they've received it. Just as you two were."

"I think that's a good place to be," Reno said, finishing off his toast. He wiped his hands on the linen napkin in his lap. "We're just a part of this entire process, not the center of it."

"I thought we were," Calen said, "but I was wrong. And that's okay. We've been corrected and things are still moving forward."

"You have all of the spheres so far that have unveiled themselves," Shelly said. "Guerra must be fuming. He only has one."

"It means Guerra is going to want the other spheres even more than ever," Reno growled. He picked up his coffee cup and drank a sip of the steaming brew. "And he's going to pull out all the stops to get it one way or another."

"Even with one sphere in his possession," Shelly said, "that stops us from stringing the necklace so that Ana can wear it and help shift the energy to the light?"

Reno nodded, before taking a sip of coffee. "That's right. We have no idea how to get that sphere out of the *Tupay* fortress in the fourth dimension. We're in talks with Grandmother Alaria and Grandfather Adaire about it. There's no way a *Taqe* can enter that fortress to steal it back. They said they might have a plan on how to get the sixth and the seventh ones."

"Wow," Shelly said, "that's good news. And even if we retrieve the rest of the spheres, the necklace is still incomplete. And then we're at a stalemate?"

"You got it," Calen said. "Until we can somehow get that sphere back, the necklace won't work. Each sphere carries a certain type of energy. You can liken them to tumblers that will open a safe. Only, the safe is a powerful change of energy from heavy to light. The emeralds have to be strung in the order that we find them. Then Ana can wear the necklace and the new energy be brought online in our world to help all of us here to move from *Tupay* to the lighter, more positive energy of the *Taqe*."

"That's awful that you've lost one of them," Shelly said, sprinkling a bit of brown sugar across her bowl of steel-cut oatmeal. "I honestly didn't realize until now the importance of the seven spheres."

"What's awful is that we lost Robert Cramer." Calen gave her husband a sad look. "That's a weight we carry. We should never have asked him on that mission. He just didn't have the paranormal skills that were needed."

Reaching out, Reno covered his wife's hand.

"Stop torturing yourself over this, Calen. We're not perfect. Nothing down here is. We did the best we could. Yes, we made a mistake. And, yes, we did learn from it." Reno looked at Colt and Shelly. "The universal intelligence is going directly to people who have the right skills to find the next emerald. That's not such a bad deal."

"I know, but it hurts to know that we put Robert in the line of fire and he wasn't really prepared for it," Calen lamented.

Shelly reached over and touched Colt's hand. "It took everything we had as a team to find it. Colt and I complemented one another with our skills. I couldn't have found that sphere by myself."

Colt squeezed her fingers. Shelly, in a bright red T-shirt and white linen trousers, looked beautiful. Her hair, once mussed, was tamed into place, a frame for her glorious hazel eyes that shone with such love for him. "The Great Spirit chose the right two people," he agreed, a catch in his tone.

Reno nodded. He wiped his mouth and put his napkin back into place across his massive lap. "Well, before you leave this evening for home," he told Colt, "we would like you to complete your mission report."

"I'm almost done with it. I'll hand it in to you before I leave," Colt promised. For now, he had most of this day with Shelly. He would miss her terribly.

The coming week he'd be back on his reservation in order to change his life. Looking deeply into her sparkling hazel eyes, Colt felt his heart lift. Hope infused him as never before. When he returned to the foundation, he would be returning with a wedding ring and asking her to marry him. That was something he was looking forward to—a future with this courageous young woman. Colt would love her forever.

* * * * *

Don't miss Lindsay McKenna's next book,
GUARDIAN, *available June 2010*
from Silhouette Nocturne.

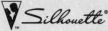

HARLEQUIN® *Romance*®

GIRLS' *Weekend in* VEGAS

Four friends, four dream weddings!

On a girly weekend in Las Vegas, best friends Alex, Molly,
Serena and Jayne are supposed to just have fun and forget
men, but they end up meeting their perfect matches!
Will the love they find in Vegas stay in Vegas?

Find out in this sassy, fun and wildly romantic miniseries
all about love and friendship!

Saving Cinderella! by MYRNA MACKENZIE
Available June

Vegas Pregnancy Surprise by SHIRLEY JUMP
Available July

Inconveniently Wed! by JACKIE BRAUN
Available August

Wedding Date with the Best Man
by MELISSA MCCLONE
Available September

www.eHarlequin.com

HRI7663

From *USA TODAY* bestselling author

LEANNE BANKS

CEO'S EXPECTANT SECRETARY

Elle Linton is hiding more than just her affair
with her boss Brock Maddox. And she's
terrifed that if their secret turns public her
mother's life may be put at risk. When she
unexpectedly becomes pregnant she's forced
to make a decision. Will she be able to save
her relationship and her mother's life?

*Available June
wherever books are sold.*

Always Powerful, Passionate and Provocative.

SD73031

HARLEQUIN
Ambassadors

Want to share your passion for reading Harlequin® Books?

Become a Harlequin Ambassador!

Harlequin Ambassadors are a group of passionate and well-connected readers who are willing to share their joy of reading Harlequin® books with family and friends.

You'll be sent all the tools you need to spark great conversation, including free books!

All we ask is that you share the romance with your friends and family!

You'll also be invited to have a say in new book ideas and exchange opinions with women just like you!

To see if you qualify* to be a Harlequin Ambassador, please visit
www.HarlequinAmbassadors.com.

*Please note that not everyone who applies to be a Harlequin Ambassador will qualify. For more information please visit www.HarlequinAmbassadors.com.

Thank you for your participation.

HARLEQUIN® *Blaze*™

is proud to present

New York Times bestselling author

Vicki Lewis Thompson

with a brand-new trilogy,
SONS OF CHANCE
where three sexy brothers
meet three irresistible women.

Look for the first book
WANTED!

*Available beginning in June 2010
wherever books are sold.*

---

red-hot reads

www.eHarlequin.com

HB79548

REQUEST YOUR
FREE BOOKS!
2 FREE NOVELS PLUS 2 FREE GIFTS!

Silhouette®

nocturne™

Dramatic and Sensual Tales of Paranormal Romance.

YES! Please send me 2 FREE Silhouette® Nocturne™ novels and my 2 FREE gifts (gifts are worth about $10). After receiving them, if I don't wish to receive any more books, I can return the shipping statement marked "cancel." If I don't cancel, I will receive 4 brand-new novels every other month and be billed just $4.47 per book in the U.S. or $4.99 per book in Canada. That's a saving of at least 15% off the cover price! It's quite a bargain! Shipping and handling is just 50¢ per book.* I understand that accepting the 2 free books and gifts places me under no obligation to buy anything. I can always return a shipment and cancel at any time. Even if I never buy another book from Silhouette, the two free books and gifts are mine to keep forever.

238/338 SDN E5QS

Name _____ (PLEASE PRINT)

Address _____ Apt. #

City _____ State/Prov. _____ Zip/Postal Code

Signature (if under 18, a parent or guardian must sign)

Mail to the Silhouette Reader Service:
IN U.S.A.: P.O. Box 1867, Buffalo, NY 14240-1867
IN CANADA: P.O. Box 609, Fort Erie, Ontario L2A 5X3

Not valid for current subscribers to Silhouette Nocturne books.

Want to try two free books from another line?
Call 1-800-873-8635 or visit www.morefreebooks.com.

* Terms and prices subject to change without notice. Prices do not include applicable taxes. N.Y. residents add applicable sales tax. Canadian residents will be charged applicable provincial taxes and GST. Offer not valid in Quebec. This offer is limited to one order per household. All orders subject to approval. Credit or debit balances in a customer's account(s) may be offset by any other outstanding balance owed by or to the customer. Please allow 4 to 6 weeks for delivery. Offer available while quantities last.

Your Privacy: Silhouette is committed to protecting your privacy. Our Privacy Policy is available online at www.eHarlequin.com or upon request from the Reader Service. From time to time we make our lists of customers available to reputable third parties who may have a product or service of interest to you. If you would prefer we not share your name and address, please check here. ☐

Help us get it right—We strive for accurate, respectful and relevant communications. To clarify or modify your communication preferences, visit us at www.ReaderService.com/consumerchoice.

SN10R